Plain Jane Takes Back Her Name

AMF Publishing

Allison Felten

PLAIN JANE TAKES BACK HER NAME

Proofreading & edits done by Emily LeVault.

Illustrations done by James Warwood.

Cover design by Allison Felten.

ISBN: 979-8-9891732-4-2 (paperback)

First Paperback Edition, 2024

To all the awkward kids navigating through the maze of middle school. Find your path one step at a time. You've got this!

September

September 1st

Hey there, Diary!

I'm an 11-year-old with brown hair that's always finding its way into a messy ponytail, and these brown eyes that have a knack for curiosity. I stand at 4' 10'' (which I hear is pretty average) but I swear, I'm still growing!

Here's a little about me: I'm a fan of good books, especially mysteries. Sometimes it's nice to escape reality. Swimming's my jam— there's something freeing about gliding through the water. This summer was the first year I was on a swim team, and I loved it! It definitely showcased my competitive side. You can also find me riding my bike around the neighborhood, enjoying the breeze.

I can't believe it's already the first day of September. This summer has been an absolute whirlwind!

It started with my elementary school graduation back in June. That feels like a lifetime ago, even though it's only been a few months. I felt like a superstar walking through the gym in my cap and gown. I was surrounded by friends and family, making it a day I'll never forget!

I did feel a bit sad at the graduation because my friend Esmé is going to a different middle school. The two of us have been in the same class since third grade and it's hard to think about having a school experience without her. The good news is we've hung out a few times over the summer, and our friendship is still going strong!

In July, my cousin Dominique came to visit from the East Coast. I hadn't seen her in years, but it was like we had never been apart. We spent the entire summer together, and she quickly became my best friend.

We did everything together from joining the swim team, having movie nights, and even going on a mini road trip to the city. Dominique is so much fun, and I feel like we have a special connection that goes beyond just being cousins.

Oh, I almost forgot to mention that Dominique was the one who gave me this diary as a gift. She had this idea that we should both write in a diary throughout the next year. That way, when she comes back next summer, we can share everything that happened during sixth grade.

It's bittersweet knowing that summer is coming to an end, but I'm excited to see what the future holds.

I can't wait to fill this diary!

Jane

-x-X-x-X-x-X-x-X-x-X-x-X-x-X-x-

September 2nd

Dear Diary,

My family's a bit crazy. Dad used to be in the army, but now he's tackling a different battlefield: insurance. He's got that disciplined, no-nonsense approach from his army days, but he's also the one who'll surprise you with a hilarious joke when you least expect it.

Mom's the manager at our local grocery store. She's got this incredible knack for keeping things running smoothly, both at work and at home. She's the one who somehow manages to juggle a million things at once and still has time to whip up the best spaghetti in town.

Now, onto the chaos generators—my younger brothers, Joey and Carl. They're in fourth and second grade this year. They can be super annoying, especially when they team up against me, but I guess that's just the brotherly bond, right?

Welcome to the Alcott family!

Jane

September 3rd

Dear Diary,

I went shopping for some new school clothes, and it turned into a total rollercoaster of emotions. I was so excited at the thought of updating my wardrobe for middle school, but little did I know what I was in for...

First off, I have to say that my mom has some seriously outdated fashion taste. She kept picking out clothes with unicorns and rainbows. I mean, seriously, unicorns? It's not like I'm six years old anymore!

I wanted to get this cute crop top I saw, but my mom flat-out refused. She said it was too revealing, and that I was too young to wear something like that. Ugh, parents can be so frustrating sometimes! We ended up settling on some okay shirts—the only good one being a tie-dye t-shirt. But it's just not the same as the awesome crop top I wanted.

I swear, I had a little bit of a meltdown right there in the store. I know, it sounds totally embarrassing, and I regret losing my cool, but I couldn't help it! I just wanted to feel more grown-up and express myself through my style.

To top it all off, my two younger brothers were being incredibly annoying. They kept running off in different directions, which distracted Mom. I was about to give up on looking cool when I came up with a sneaky plan. While my mom was busy arguing with Carl about a toy he wanted, I quietly snuck the crop top into the pile of clothes. It was a risky move, but I had to try.

To my shock, when we got to the checkout counter, my mom didn't even notice the shirt. She paid for everything, and I felt like I had just won a secret battle. I can't believe she actually bought it!

I know I should feel bad about being so sneaky, but I feel like I've won a small victory. For now, I'm going to revel in the fact that I have a cool new crop top to wear to school. Maybe I'll even pair it with my cute ripped jeans.

With a sly grin,

Jane

-x-X-x-X-x-X-x-X-x-X-x-X-x-X-x-

Labor Day, September 5th

Dear Diary,

Labor Day was an absolute blast! We went over to my Uncle Randy and Aunt Sandra's house, which has a fantastic pool. It turned out to be a day filled with fun, sun, and some unexpected family bonding.

I got to hang out with my older cousins, Noah and Rebecca. They both had some of their high school friends at the party, so I felt super mature spending time with them. We spent the entire day eating good food, hanging out, and swimming. It was so much fun!

Diary, remember how I told you I joined the swim team with Dominique this summer? It turns out I'm an amazing swimmer! I was one of the fastest kids there. I definitely ended up showing off some of my amazing swimming skills at the Labor Day party.

At one point during the party, Rebecca and her friend asked me how I felt about my first day of middle school being tomorrow. I told her I was super excited and ready to dive in (pun intended) to a great year. For some reason, they shared a weird look and started giving me advice.

While I appreciated their concern, I know I'm going to fly into the next school year and have a fantastic time. I've had an incredible summer, and I have a feeling that all of this positive energy is going to follow me into sixth grade.

Ready for my first day!

Jane

10:30 PM

I should be getting some rest, but my mind is racing with thoughts of the first day of middle school. I got my schedule in the mail last week, and I've pretty much memorized it by now. I know what order my classes are in, their room numbers, my teacher's names, what time each class starts, and I've even got my school supplies packed and ready to go.

I'll try to count some imaginary sheep to help me doze off. After all, I want to be well- rested and at my best when I walk through the doors of East Oak Middle School tomorrow. Sixth grade, here I come!

September 6th

Dear Diary,

I wish I could say that my first day of middle school was a roaring success, but it was pretty much a disaster from start to finish. Everything that could go wrong, did go wrong, and I'm feeling pretty bummed right now.

It all started with a disastrous breakfast. My little brother, Joey, decided it would be a brilliant idea to spill cranberry juice all over me. The juice stained my decoy shirt, and when I went up to my room to change, I realized my secret crop top underneath was also stained. I had to rush to find a different look, which ended up being pretty basic.

I asked Mom not to walk me those two short blocks to school. Not to be mean, but I wanted a shot at feeling more independent. Still, she managed to get a classic beginning-of-the-school-year photo. You know, the one where I have to hold a sign with my name, grade, future career ambitions, and all those other odd details. So awkward...

Everything was going fine until I went inside East Oak Middle. The hallways were a chaotic mess—it was so loud, and there were way more students than I was used to from elementary school.

Despite memorizing my class schedule and room numbers, I couldn't seem to find them. It was like I had entered a labyrinth with no way out. I felt so lost, and just when I thought things couldn't get any worse, the bell for homeroom rang. Panic set in as I realized I was lost and late on my first day!

The school custodian came to my rescue and helped me find my first class, which I had apparently passed by three times before. I felt like such a little kid. My confidence took a major hit.

Once homeroom was over, I hurried to my first class, which was conveniently right next door. I arrived early, eager to get settled. To my surprise, I didn't spot anyone from my elementary school, and the teacher seemed super strict. The second class was no better. Once again, I didn't know anyone there, and to make things even more confusing, there was another girl named Jane. What are the odds, right?

But what really got on my nerves was that this other Jane was wearing the EXACT SAME crop top I was going to wear. I couldn't help but compare us, and it seemed like she looked better in it. Ugh! Why does she have to make me feel so grumpy?

During lunch, I sat at a table with kids who all had cell phones. They were talking about some viral video and laughing like crazy. I felt left out because I don't have a cell phone yet, and I've never seen the video they were talking about. I just sat there, quietly eating my food, hoping nobody would notice me.

I'm hoping that things will get better as I settle into this new school, but right now, I can't help but feel like a fish out of water.

Hoping it's a first-day fluke.

Jane

-x-X-x-X-x-X-x-X-x-X-x-X-x-X-x-

September 13th

Dear Diary,

It's been a week since I started middle school, and I can't help but feel like I'm stuck in a never-ending storm. Nothing seems to be going right, and I'm starting to doubt if things will ever get better.

One of the big revelations I had this week is that each grade is broken into three teams. I'm on the A-Team, while all my friends from elementary school are on the B and C-Teams. The A-Team is known for having the strictest teacher, and I've already felt the weight of that reputation. I've had homework every single day, even though it's only the first week!

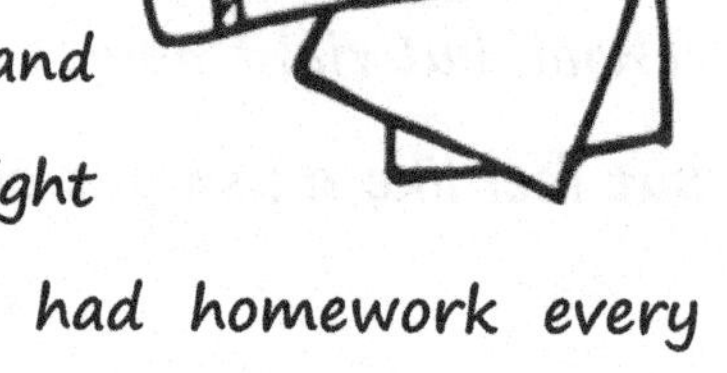

To make matters worse, the other Jane is still bothering me. We have five out of seven classes together, so I can't seem to get away from her. Since we have so many classes together, she told people to call her *Janey* to make it less confusing, but it's not like people were going to get us confused! *Janey* is tall, with blonde highlighted hair and green eyes. I'm an average height, a tiny bit chubby, and have brown hair and brown eyes.

I wish I could find my place in this new world. A place where I don't feel insignificant and insecure. Is that too much to ask for?

Plain Jane

-x-X-x-X-x-X-x-X-x-X-x-X-x-X-x-

September 16th

Dear Diary,

I finally got my locker assignment, and it turns out that students have to share lockers! It feels like there's just not enough space in this place.

I didn't know anyone to share a locker with, so my homeroom teacher paired me up randomly with a boy named Harold. I couldn't believe I'd never really noticed him until today. He's in all my classes, so you'd think I would have seen him around. He's quite skinny, wears glasses, and has messy brown hair. He's a bit unique, but overall, a nice guy.

The teacher gave us the locker combo and had us practice opening the locker a few times. Harold got it open the first time, but it took me a few tries. Luckily, he was good at explaining how to use a combination lock, and I was able to figure it out.

I was pleasantly surprised when he let me decide whether I wanted the top or bottom shelf of our locker. I picked the top because I don't want to bend over all the time, even though he is taller. Sharing a locker with Harold might not be so bad after all.

I hope I remember the locker combo...

Jane

-x-X-x-X-x-X-x-X-x-X-x-X-x-X-x-

September 17th

Dear Diary,

I'm currently at my friend Esmé's house for a sleepover, and I have to admit it's been a little overwhelming. Esmé and I were really good friends in elementary school. I was so excited when she invited me over because I hadn't seen her since the summer.

I thought it would just be the two of us, but she invited a couple of her new friends from North Pine Middle School (which happens to be East Oak's rival). The thought of hanging out with these "rivals" makes me a bit uneasy, especially considering how challenging things have been for me at my new school.

Diary... I might have told a little white lie when they asked me how sixth grade was going. I said I've made lots of friends, but the truth is, it's been far from easy. I didn't want to admit that I've been feeling pretty out of place and have been struggling to fit in.

Esmé, being the kind person that she is, said she can't wait until I have a sleepover at my place so she can meet all of my new friends. She even suggested we could make a giant friend group. I appreciate her enthusiasm, but I can't help but feel anxious about the idea.

For now, I'll focus on enjoying this sleepover. Who knows, maybe I'll even become better friends with Esmé's friends, despite our school rivalry.

Time for some sleepover fun!

Jane

September 19th

Dear Diary,

My mom found the crop top that I had sneakily added to the pile of clothes during our back-to-school shopping trip. I can't believe I forgot it was in my laundry basket!

At first, she assumed that I had stolen it. I felt my heart sink as she looked at me like a criminal. I quickly explained that it was in the pile of clothes we bought, but she wasn't convinced. She pulled up the digital receipt on her phone. I thought she would be less mad when she saw it on the receipt. I was wrong.

The fact that I had been so sneaky and had gone against her wishes infuriated her. She told me that I had not only disobeyed her but also broken her trust. The punishment came quickly—I was grounded from my tablet for two weeks.

I know I shouldn't have been sneaky, and I definitely regret it now. It feels like the punishment is a bit harsh, but I understand that I made a mistake. I hope to learn from it and rebuild my mom's trust. In the meantime, I'll have to find other ways to entertain myself without my tablet.

Caught red-handed.

Jane

September 29th

Dear Diary,

I'm sorry for not writing in you for such a long time. Time just slipped by. Things haven't gotten worse, but they also haven't gotten better. Middle school continues to be challenging, and I'm still struggling.

The one bright spot in all of this is that I've become friends with Harold. It's mostly because we're together in all our classes, but he's turning out to be a pretty good listener.

However, there's one thing that's been driving me crazy. It's become painfully obvious that Harold has a major crush on *Janey*. It's not like I have a crush on Harold or anything, I just don't like the fact that out of all the girls, he is attracted to the other Jane.

Totally annoyed.

Jane

October

October 8th

Dear Diary,

I can't believe I'm actually writing this down, but I have to tell someone, even if it's just you. I've been keeping this secret for a while now. I have a crush, and it's no ordinary crush—I'm in love! His name is Benji Bullara.

Benji is absolutely amazing. He's tall with dark brown hair and the most mesmerizing blue eyes I've ever seen. I can't help but get lost in them. He's also on the cross-country team and does robotics. Athletic and smart!

Yesterday, I stayed after school to watch him at the home cross-country race. To be honest, it was kind of boring. You could only see a few parts of the trail where the kids were running, and it wasn't as exciting as I thought it would be.

When I told Harold about my plans to watch the race, he volunteered to stay after school to keep me company. I'm really glad he stayed because talking with him passed the time. We chatted about classes, our elementary schools, the cross-country meet, and even our hobbies. It's not like we're best friends or anything, but it's good to have someone to hang out with.

I just hope I can find a way to get to know Benji better, or at least get close enough to him to find out if he likes me back. But for now, I'll just keep admiring him from a distance, and maybe, someday, I'll gather the courage to talk to him.

Here's to the thrilling possibility of love.

Jane

-x-X-x-X-x-X-x-X-x-X-x-X-x-X-x-

October 15th

Dear Diary,

Progress reports were sent home, and it turns out I'm failing my Social Studies class. My parents were furious when they saw the grade last night, and I had to endure a long lecture about the importance of my education.

The thing is, it's not like I want to fail. It's just that my Social Studies teacher makes the class so boring. All we do is read chapters out of the textbook and answer questions. It's monotonous, and my hand always cramps up from writing.

My parents decided to restrict my time on the tablet to just one hour each day. That's barely enough time to do anything! This is so unfair! They said that if I manage to bring my grade up to a B, they'll take off the time limit.

This morning, before school started, I talked with my Social Studies teacher. She offered to give me some extra homework to improve my grade.

At the time, it seemed like a good idea, but now I'm starting to regret it. I've got twice as much work to do, and it feels like I'm drowning in assignments. To make matters more frustrating, I found out that Harold is getting an A in the same class. I'm going to talk to him and see if he'd be up for helping me with some of the Social Studies work.

Unwilling history buff,

Jane

October 20th

Dear Diary,

Today, the school announced a big Halloween dance, and I'm super pumped about it! Halloween is one of my favorite holidays, and I've been waiting for something like this to come along. It's the perfect opportunity to let loose and make a name for myself.

During lunch, I talked to Harold, who mentioned that he wanted to wear his taco costume for the dance. I couldn't help but think it's so random and doesn't make any sense. I mean, it's a fun idea, but I'm not sure it's the best choice for middle school.

During my math class, I overheard some of the popular girls talking about their Halloween costumes. They want to go as Halloween classics like witches, vampires, and mummies but with a twist—they're getting skimpy costumes that show a lot of skin. How do they get their parents to agree to buy those costumes?

All their talk got me thinking that I should get a cute new costume so I can fit in a bit more. It's the perfect chance to make a good impression and maybe even ask Benji to dance.

Diary, I've been feeling like an outsider all year. Maybe this is my chance to change that. I'm going to put extra effort into picking out a costume and getting ready for the dance. Here's to embracing the spirit of Halloween and making a fresh start.

Your cutie black cat, ghost, or...whatever!

Jane

-x-X-x-X-x-X-x-X-x-X-x-X-x-X-x-

October 22nd

Dear Diary,

I had the most amazing idea today! I'm set on making an impression at the Halloween dance, and I've come up with a plan that I think will not only impress everyone but also make me feel like I finally belong.

So, here's the deal: I convinced Harold to do a dance with me to the popular song "Big Up" by Cheer Grenade. When the song plays, Harold and I will break out into our dance and totally blow everyone away! The song is upbeat and with a killer dance routine, we'll become instant stars of the night.

But that's not all. I managed to persuade Harold to go shopping with me this weekend so we can pick out cool costumes. I can tell he's not entirely on board with my plan, but we have to make this work. I need this.

I can't wait to go shopping for the perfect costume and start planning our dance.

It's time to dress to impress!

Jane

-x-X-x-X-x-X-x-X-x-X-x-X-x-X-x

October 24th

Dear Diary,

Today, my dad and I met up with Harold and his parents for a shopping trip to the Halloween store. I was hoping to find the perfect costume for the Halloween dance, but it turned out to be a bit of a challenge.

I first spotted a cute genie outfit that I thought would be perfect, but my dad immediately shot it down. He said it was too revealing. I then tried suggesting a nurse outfit, thinking it could be a fun costume, but my dad said no again. It felt like every suggestion I had was met with disapproval.

Then Harold came over with a pizza costume. He said if I was a pizza, he could still go as a taco. He thought it would be hilarious, and surprisingly, my dad agreed. I was mortified!

At the end of our shopping trip, the only thing my dad was willing to buy me was a lame purple cutie-bear onesie... It's not exactly what I had envisioned for the dance, but I guess I can make the best of it. Harold also agreed to get a blue cutie-bear onesie to match. The saving grace in

all of this is that the cutie-bear costumes will look cool with our dance routine.

After shopping, we grabbed some pizza and then went to Harold's house, which is *gigantic*! I couldn't believe how spacious and cool his house was. After we finished the pizza, we went to hang out in his rec room, which had a giant projector, a pool table, and even a little kitchen area. It's like a dream hangout spot!

We decided to use the projector to play the "Big Up" music video so we could plan and practice our dance. It was so much fun!

Even though our costumes are unconventional, I'm starting to think that they're going to add to the humor of our performance. I can't wait for the Halloween dance, and I'm feeling more and more excited.

Your cutie-bear,

Jane

October 25th

Dear Diary,

I arrived home from school today to find my mom video chatting with her sister, my Aunt Val. I couldn't help but jump in and take over the conversation because my cousin Dominique was also there.

I asked her how her sixth-grade year has been going and she said it's been amazing so far. She's part of the popular group and feels like she rules the school. Hearing that made me embarrassed that I've struggled to feel like I fit in. I played it off by focusing on the upcoming Halloween dance. I told her about my costume and the dance routine I've been working on. She seemed a little envious because her school hasn't had a dance yet.

I've got to focus on finding where I fit in...

Jane

October 28th

Dear Diary,

It's the day before the dance, and I can hardly contain my excitement! Harold has come over to my house every day after school since it's so close. I have to say, we're feeling pretty confident about our performance!

But the real big news happened in my science class. The teacher was pairing students up to look at different types of cells through microscopes and I was paired with Benji!

I was nervous, so we mostly talked about the assignment but I did take the opportunity to ask Benji if he was going to the dance. He said, "Yeah, I'll be there." It was a simple exchange, but it felt way deeper. I can't help but think that Benji might dance with me!

I'm so excited about the possibilities for tomorrow night. I have my cutie-bear costume hanging up, and my dance routine is ready!

Soon I'll be dancing with the stars!

Jane

-x-X-x-X-x-X-x-X-x-X-x-X-x-X-x

October 29th

Dear Diary,

I can barely find the words to write about what happened tonight. It's too embarrassing, but I need to get it out. The Halloween dance was... something else.

The gym looked incredible, with the lights dimmed, fog rolling across the floor, and an array of laser lights creating a spooky atmosphere. The school even got a professional DJ!

As soon as I got to the dance I met up with Harold. People were still trickling in, so we decided to hang out at the snack table for a while. The school went all out with the treats, and my favorite part was the chocolate fountain! It was a fun and delicious way to start the evening.

Next, Harold and I ended up playing tag and running around with some other kids. It was honestly super fun to just goof off. But then, the good music started playing, and people began to dance. That's when my nerves began to set in.

I couldn't help but notice the popular kids in their mature costumes, dancing like pros. *Janey*, of course, looked amazing as a creepy doll. It was super annoying how Harold's attention kept wandering over to her. Ugh!

Then I saw Benji. Diary, you won't believe this, but he was dressed up as a TACO! When Harold saw that, he glared at me, but he was too nice to say anything. I kept telling myself not to be nervous, and to ask Benji to dance, but with each passing song, it seemed harder to do. I was about to give up on the idea when "Big Up" came on. I figured I could do my routine, gain some confidence, and then ask Benji for the next dance.

Harold and I went to the middle of the dance floor. We started doing our routine, and the other students began creating a circle around us. For a moment, everything was amazing! People were laughing and cheering, and a few kids even pulled out their phones to record. I began to feel like I was making an impact, and everyone was finally seeing me.

But right before the big finale, *it* happened.

I bent over for a dance move and heard a giant rip. Then, I felt a cool breeze on my backside. My costume had ripped from the middle of the back down my left leg, and everyone saw my underwear! Look, I know I should've worn something underneath the cutie-bear costume, but it was so hot, and I thought it would be fine.

I couldn't get off the dance floor fast enough! I ran to the bathroom and locked myself in a stall. I told myself not to cry, but I still did. I felt so much like a baby, but I couldn't help it! This was the worst night ever!

I managed to sneak to the front office and call my mom. I explained that my costume ripped, and I needed her to come get me. I think she could tell how upset I was because she drove right over even though we live so close to the school.

Diary, I'm embarrassed beyond words! I certainly have made an impression at school, but it's not good. I don't know how I'll face everyone on Monday.

What should I do?

Jane

Halloween, October 31st

Dear Diary,

Today is Halloween. In the past it's been a day I looked forward to, but this year, it just doesn't feel the same.

After everything that happened at the dance, I'm not in the mood for trick-or- treating. The thought of putting on a costume felt too daunting. Instead, I put on a coat and took my little brothers out to trick-or-treat.

Joey was dressed up like a ninja, and Carl was dressed up like a football player. Seeing them take on their characters was nice, but I still felt a bit sad. I think my brothers could tell I wasn't in the best mood, because when we got home, they each gave me a handful of candy.

I want to find a way to bounce back and regain my confidence. But for now, I'm left feeling empty and disappointed.

Maybe one more piece of candy wouldn't hurt...

Jane

November

November 1st

Dear Diary,

Today marked my first day back at school after the dance disaster. As I walked through the hallways, I couldn't help but notice the occasional whispers and sidelong glances, but nobody said anything directly to me.

The first thing Harold did when he saw me was hug me. I wasn't expecting it, but it did make me feel better. He told me he was sorry that my costume ripped. I played it off and told him it was no big deal, but we both knew it was...

In math class, *Janey* came over to my desk. I thought she was going to be mean, but to my surprise, she was incredibly nice. She asked if I was okay after the dance. Once again, I played it cool.

I was surprised my classmates handled the "cutie-bear tear" in a mature way. But, their maturity doesn't stop me from still feeling mortified. I don't know... maybe I can find my way back to feeling more comfortable and confident at school.

Keeping my head down.

Jane

-x-X-x-X-x-X-x-X-x-X-x-X-x-X-x-

November 8th

Dear Diary,

It feels like the chaos of the cutie-bear dance fiasco has finally started to fade from people's memories. I'm starting to feel a little less self-conscious at school, which is a relief.

But the real reason I wanted to write is because something exciting happened today! I found out the robotics team is looking for new members because some students dropped out. Why would I be interested in joining robotics? Two words: Benji Bullara!

The only problem is that I was a little bit nervous to join by myself. After a bit of persuasion, I managed to talk Harold into signing up with me. No matter what happens with Benji, it'll be nice to spend time with a friend.

I can't wait for our first meeting! I have a feeling this could be a chance to explore a different side of school life and maybe even discover new passions (or relationships).

Your soon-to-be engineering expert!

Jane

-x-X-x-X-x-X-x-X-x-X-x-X-x-X-x-

November 10th

Dear Diary,

Today was my first robotics meeting, and I'll be honest; it was overwhelming. I've never coded or built robots before, and everyone seemed so knowledgeable. I was fighting to keep up.

Harold, on the other hand, took to robotics quickly. Not only is he a natural at coding, but he's getting along with the team so easily. I'm glad he's there, but I can't deny feeling a little bit jealous. I wish I could be as naturally good as he is.

At one point I was struggling and Benji came to the rescue. He was really patient as he showed me what was wrong with my code, and how to adjust it. With his guidance, I can now make the robot perform some basic functions—move forward, backward, rotate, raise its arm, and even make some funny sounds. It's amazing how much you can do with a little bit of code!

After Benji helped me, he ended up busy programming a mission for the competition in January. Watching him work was mesmerizing; he's so skilled and focused.

If things keep going well, I think I'll ask Benji out before winter break. I hope I can muster up the courage to do it!

Ready for robotics and romance.

Jane

-x-X-x-X-x-X-x-X-x-X-x-X-x-X-x-

Veterans Day, November 11th

Dear Diary,

Today was Veterans Day, a day to honor and remember those who served. It's always a meaningful day for my family, especially because my dad served in the army before he became an insurance broker.

We attended a candlelight vigil at the local community center in honor of veterans. It was an emotional ceremony, and I found myself getting pretty teary-eyed. It's hard not to when you realize the sacrifices people have made for our country.

However, halfway through the vigil, my brothers started their usual antics, poking and teasing each other. It kind of broke the emotional intensity, and I couldn't help being super annoyed. Sometimes they just don't know how to act.

After the ceremony, things got a little brighter. I bumped into Esmé and another friend from elementary school named Sam. Both of them go to North Pine Middle School, so it was fun to catch up and reminisce on the good ol' days.

The only thing that made me a little nervous was Esmé brought up the sleepover I said I'd have with all of my "new friends". I told her I'd ask my parents when I could do that, but I don't think I will. I quickly changed the subject and from that point on, the rest of the event went smoothly.

Thankful for all of the veterans,

Jane

-x-X-x-X-x-X-x-X-x-X-x-X-x-X-x-

November 17th

Dear Diary,

Today at lunch, something unexpected happened. Benji invited Harold and me to sit with him! I was so excited to eat lunch with him, but it turned out that most of the conversation revolved around robotics. I felt like I didn't have much to contribute. It doesn't matter much

because I'm not sure if I'll be invited again due to what happened at robotics practice...

At the practice after school, the team captain, Gia, was working on a crucial mission where the robot had to push a rollercoaster car up an incline. It was the final mission, and the pressure was high. Gia asked me to make a modification, adding a 90-degree rotation to the end of the code.

And then disaster struck. In my attempt to add the rotation, I accidentally deleted the entire code! It felt like time stood still as I realized what I had done. The team was relying on that code for the mission, and I had wiped it all out.

I apologized profusely, but the damage was done. The team was understandably frustrated, and the captain had to start coding from scratch. The teacher said it was everyone's fault because we should have been saving the code as we worked, but still, I felt terrible.

I hope I can make it up somehow and regain the team's trust. It was an honest mistake, but it felt like a huge setback.

Messing up at every turn.

Jane

-x-X-x-X-x-X-x-X-x-X-x-X-x-X-x-

November 18th

Dear Diary,

Today was tough. Throughout the school day, Gia and some other members of the robotics team kept giving me ice-cold glares. I could tell they were still upset that I had deleted the code. I found myself seriously considering quitting.

I confided in Harold and told him I wanted to leave the team. Without a second thought, he insisted that I stay. He assured me that my mistake wasn't as big of a problem as the others were making it out to be. His support surprised me, but I'm not sure why. Harold has turned out to be my best friend at East Oak Middle School.

So, despite my doubts and the lingering embarrassment from yesterday, I've decided to stick it out. It's not an easy decision, but I'll try to find the silver lining in all of this.

I'm not done yet.

Jane

-x-X-x-X-x-X-x-X-x-X-x-X-x-X-x-

November 23rd

Dear Diary,

Today was the day before Thanksgiving break and the school dropped a bombshell: a winter pageant is in the works! Auditions are right after the break. I'm thrilled, but also nervous about it.

The pageant was written by the music teacher. It follows a boy and girl traveling through a winter wonderland. As they travel, the students

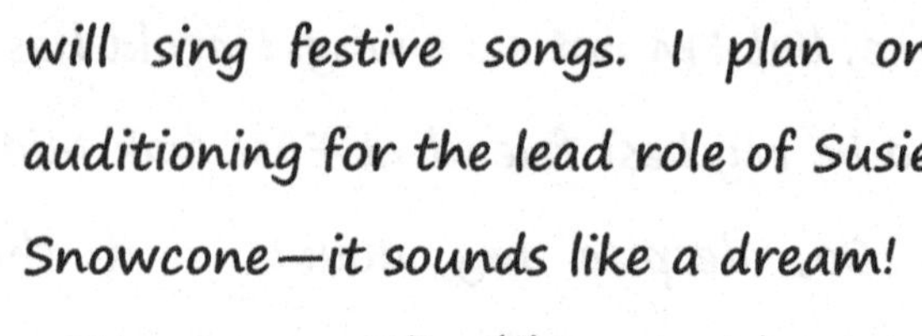

will sing festive songs. I plan on auditioning for the lead role of Susie Snowcone—it sounds like a dream!

Now comes the dilemma: I have to pick a song for the audition. There are so many holiday songs to choose from, and I want to make sure I pick one that showcases my voice.

I've been practicing a few different songs in my room, trying to find the one that feels right. It's going to be hard work, but I'm determined to nail the audition.

I'm excited but also a little jittery about the whole process. The last time I performed on stage was at my fifth-grade graduation, and even then I was with my class. Performing solo is a whole different level! Fingers crossed that I can impress the music teacher with whatever song I go with.

Your leading lady,

Jane

Thanksgiving, November 25th

Dear Diary,

Thanksgiving is here! I slept in until 11 AM, which felt like such a treat. I could have slept another two hours if Joey and Carl hadn't burst into my room and woken me up. Total brats!

I went downstairs and was met with the delicious aroma of my dad's green bean casserole cooking. I don't really like green beans, but there's something about my dad's casserole!

At 4 o'clock my family drove to Uncle Randy and Aunt Sandra's house. The best part? Reconnecting with my older cousins Rebecca and Noah. As soon as we got there, it was hugs and high-fives all around.

As we settled in for Thanksgiving dinner, the table was a sight to behold. The array of dishes—turkey, mashed potatoes, stuffing, cranberry sauce—had my mouth watering in anticipation. I made sure to leave some room for that green bean casserole, and it didn't disappoint. The warmth of the gathering and the chatter around the table made the meal taste even better. We all shared stories, laughed, and enjoyed every bite of the delicious food.

Then, cue the gaming extravaganza! My brothers, cousins and I parked ourselves around the TV and dove into this epic racing game. It was intense! We were competing for bragging rights like our lives depended on it.

And oh, the entertainment didn't stop there. Noah whipped out his phone, and suddenly, we were watching the funniest videos known to the internet. It was a cascade of giggles and snorts as we clicked from one hilarious clip to the next.

But the cherry on top? We convinced my little brothers to do a dance for a silly video. Let's just say, the internet might never be ready.

My cousin Rebecca found time to check in with me. I confessed that it's been a bit of a rough ride. She was incredibly reassuring, sharing her own experiences and reminding me that tough times in middle school are pretty common. It felt good to have someone who's been there and survived it all.

Time for a food coma.

Jane

November 28th

Dear Diary,

The last few days of break have been refreshing. I made the most of it by diving into a couple of books. There's something about a good mystery that just draws you in, don't you think?

I also had a chance to rewatch my all-time favorite TV series The Wacky Witch. It was like visiting old friends; each episode felt familiar yet as exciting as the first time I watched it. I needed that comforting nostalgia.

Now, onto the thing that has really been stressing me out. Auditions for the winter pageant are looming, and I've been working hard on perfecting my audition song. After much contemplation, I settled on "Silent Night" because I feel like it showcases my voice.

I hope my preparation pays off during auditions. It's

nerve-wracking, but I'm feeling more confident with each practice session. Fingers crossed that I'll land Susie Snowcone.

Hoping "Silent Night" puts me on stage.

Jane

-x-X-x-X-x-X-x-X-x-X-x-X-x-X-x-

November 29th

Dear Diary,

Today was the day of auditions for the winter pageant, and it didn't go as well as I hoped. I was a bundle of nerves when it was my turn to sing. Everything seemed fine until I hit the high notes, and my voice cracked. After that happened, I could feel my confidence slipping away as I finished singing.

To add salt to the wound, *Janey* went right after me. She performed a perfect rendition of "Frosty the Snowman" with a little dance routine. It felt like she effortlessly stole the spotlight.

I've been practicing and rehearsing so much, but when the moment came, my nerves got the better of me. It's frustrating, and I can't help but feel disappointed in myself.

The teacher will put up the cast list tomorrow morning. I'm hoping that she can see past my mistake and see the performer inside me. I know I could do an amazing performance if I got a chance.

Keeping my fingers crossed!

Jane

-x-X-x-X-x-X-x-X-x-X-x-X-x-X-x-

November 30th

Dear Diary,

The cast list for the winter pageant went up, and I didn't get the lead role of Susie Snowcone. I'm absolutely crushed! It might seem silly to be this upset over a school pageant, but I had my heart set on that lead role.

To make matters worse, *Janey* landed the part I wanted. I can't deny I'm jealous about that. Donte Holmes, a boy I barely know, ended up getting the male lead of Iggy Icicle.

Me? I got cast as a cup of hot chocolate. It's a small part, and my only line is, "Let me cool down!" What stings the most is that I won't have to attend rehearsals until the day before the performance because my part is so minor.

Diary, I've been in middle school for almost four months and I still feel like an outcast. To make it worse, *Janey* is taking everything I want!

Why is 6th grade so hard?

Jane

December

December 1st

Dear Diary,

I'm still pretty sad about not getting the lead, but there's nothing I can do now. I'll just do my best as a cute cup of hot chocolate!

In other news, today was the first robotics practice since the code-deleting incident. Gia kept me away from the main robot, which was a bit disappointing. I really do want to help the team.

On the bright side, I was able to work on an older robot model. I feel like I learned twice as much being able to explore the programming on my own. It's challenging, but I'm finding my way around it.

Hoping to code my way into Gia's favor!

Jane

December 1st

Dear Diary,

Harold surprised me today by inviting me to celebrate Hanukkah with his family tomorrow night. I'm a bit nervous because I don't know much about Hanukkah, but I'm eager to embrace this opportunity and learn about it.

Ready to party!

Jane

-x-X-x-X-x-X-x-X-x-X-x-X-x-X-x-

December 4th

Dear Diary,

Tonight was the night I went to Harold's house to celebrate Hanukkah. Mom insisted I dress up and, of course, the dress she picked was pretty but incredibly uncomfortable. Ugh, fashion can be so annoying sometimes!

Stepping into Harold's house was like entering a different world, in the best way possible. There were beautiful decorations and the smell of delicious food filled the air. I never knew how big Harold's extended family is! There had to be at least thirty people. His giant house almost felt cramped.

We lit the candles on the menorah, and they recited blessings and prayers in Hebrew. I learned that each night they add another candle until all eight are lit. It was really beautiful.

And the food! I've never had latkes or sufganiyot (I definitely had to look up how to spell that) before. Latkes are these amazing potato pancakes, crispy on the outside and soft on the inside, and sufganiyot are these delectable jelly-filled doughnuts. I may have eaten a few too many!

The best part, though, was spending time with Harold and his family. They made me feel so included. I even helped them play a game called Dreidel, which was super fun.

It's moments like these that remind me how lucky I am to have a friend like Harold. Without him, I wouldn't be able to survie middle school!

Happy Hanukkah!

Jane

-x-X-x-X-x-X-x-X-x-X-x-X-x-X-x-

December 6th

Dear Diary,

During homeroom, I got called down to the counselor's office. I was wracking my brain, thinking, what did I do wrong? It turned out to be something totally unexpected.

The counselor asked if I could show a new student named Alejandra around. She's got long black hair and these adorable dimples. She moved to our small town from Austin, Texas. I can't imagine what it must be like moving so far.

We have the same schedule which is why I was assigned to guide her around the school. She seemed super nice when I introduced her to Harold. Who knows? Maybe we can end up being good friends.

East Oak's newest tour guide,

Jane

December 7th

Dear Diary,

Remember when I told you about how I'm failing social studies? Well, my grade skyrocketed to 81% after my last test and all that extra homework.

When I showed Mom and Dad, they took off the time limit on my tablet. I've spent all night watching the latest viral videos.

Glad to be out of the stone age.

Jane

-x-X-x-X-x-X-x-X-x-X-x-X-x-X-x-

December 10th

Dear Diary,

Alejandra, Harold, and I have been getting along amazingly the last few days. Alejandra even brought homemade tamales for us the three of us! I'd never tried them before, and wow, they were incredible!

As we were eating the tamales, a group of popular kids behind us started laughing loudly. Alejandra rolled her eyes and said she thinks Janey and her friends are annoying. I know that shouldn't have made me happy, but it did. All I said was that they are being too loud, and should be more considerate of others. Harold didn't say anything.

Despite that, I'm starting to feel like the three of us could make a pretty awesome trio. Alejandra's fitting in so well. It's like she's been here forever. I never thought I'd be part of a best-friend group, but hey, life's full of surprises!

One of the three musketeers!

Jane

December 12th

Dear Diary,

Today was a disaster. While working on the hot chocolate outfit for the pageant, Mom and I got into a huge fight. I stormed off to my room, filled with anger I couldn't control. In a fit of frustration, I did something I shouldn't have—I cut my hair.

I hid in my room, but Mom eventually found me to try on the costume. When she saw what I did, she was furious. We argued more, and to fix the uneven mess I created, she had to cut it even shorter. I now have an ugly bob! I don't even know how to face anyone at school.

I wish I could take it all back.

Jane

-x-X-x-X-x-X-x-X-x-X-x-X-x-X-x-

December 13th

Dear Diary,

Today was tough.

I tried wearing a hat to school, hoping to hide what I did to my hair. Of course, the school has a stupid no-hat policy, so my homeroom teacher forced me to take it off.

Harold's reaction said it all—he was speechless. Alejandra hid her shock better and complimented me, saying I looked mature. Her kindness helped, even if I knew it was just to make me feel better.

A few other kids glanced at me, but no one said a word... at least to my face. It feels like the cutie-bear fiasco all over again!

I really don't know why I cut my hair in anger. It was like I lost my mind and was acting on impulse! Now I have to live with the ugly consequences of my actions.

Wanting to hide under a rock.

Jane

-x-X-x-X-x-X-x-X-x-X-x-X-x-X-x-

December 17th

Dear Diary,

Tonight was the winter pageant, and the truth is, like everything else in my life, it didn't go well. *Janey*—always perfectly poised and seemingly excelling at everything—nailed her role as Susie Snowcone. I couldn't help but feel a pang of envy as I watched her effortlessly command the stage, delivering her lines flawlessly.

My own performance was far from ideal. I lost track of time and missed my cue. The ensuing silence felt never-ending, and to my mortification, it was *Janey* who discreetly mouthed my line to me. It was a humbling experience, to say the least.

Post-pageant, there was this awkward mingling with cookies and juice. Everyone was chatting and laughing, but I was lost in thought, still replaying my flubbed moment. Harold, being the amazing friend he is, started doing this goofy dance and singing one of our holiday songs. It definitely cheered me up.

Then, another small glimmer of hope. My parents met and talked with Alejandra's folks, and somehow, we now have a New Year's Eve sleepover planned! The thought of welcoming in the new year with my new friend Alejandra and my ever-energetic bestie Esmé—gives me something to look forward to.

I am absolutely exhausted after this evening's performance, but thankfully winter break is here!

Time for some rest.

Jane

-x-X-x-X-x-X-x-X-x-X-x-X-x-X-x-

December 21st

Dear Diary,

Winter break has been treating me like royalty! Sleeping in late, curling up with books, and scrolling mindlessly on my tablet... I can't ask for more.

What's been a real surprise is how great it's been hanging out with my brothers. I usually get annoyed with them after ten minutes, but winter break magic is at work! We've played a ninja games, have been coloring, and just goofing off... something we don't usually do.

Sure, they're still a bit annoying at times, but sharing laughs with them has been refreshing. Maybe we're all just relaxing into the break, and it feels good.

Hoping this winter wonderland never ends!

Jane

-x-X-x-X-x-X-x-X-x-X-x-X-x-X-x-

Christmas Eve, December 24th

Dear Diary,

Christmas Eve was at our place this year and boy! Was it lively! It started with Uncle Randy, Aunt Sandra, and my cousins coming over. Then my grandparents on my mom's side arrived. They drove hours to get here, and are staying five days. It'll be nice to get some time with Gigi and Pops!

This year my mom decided against a traditional Christmas dinner. She kept going on about how she refused to cook another turkey.

She switched it up with lasagna, garlic bread, soup, and salad. It was maybe a little too fantastic considering the four slices of garlic bread I devoured. But hey, who could resist?

While hanging out with my cousins, Noah had some unexpected wisdom. I told him how I was still struggling in school. He pointed out that everybody is figuring it out at the beginning of sixth grade. The second part of the year is way more important because this is when people settle in. His words stuck with me—making a mark in middle school suddenly felt like a challenge I was eager to tackle.

Reflecting on Noah's advice, I'm determined to find my place and truly establish myself. I long to be Jane—not just another face in the crowd.

Sounds like the new year will be a new start.

Jane

Christmas Day, December 25th

Dear Diary,

Christmas morning had its usual fanfare. Joey and Carl burst into my room, full of excitement about Santa's visit. A part of me wished for a few more moments of shut-eye, but it became evident that the household was in a gift-unwrapping frenzy.

I had high hopes for my Christmas list, which was full of things I'd been eyeing for a while. Music gift cards were at the top, followed closely by a cell phone (which, to my dismay, didn't make an appearance), some cute crop tops, makeup to experiment with my look, and a fresh pair of shoes to strut around in.

The unwrapping was a mixed bag. There was the coveted gift card to Music Mania, a win in my book. Then came a cozy pajama set, perfect for these chilly winter nights. I also got a cute hoodie with an adorable melty happy face. But beyond that, it was a slew of presents more fitting for younger kids—stuffed animals and board games galore.

While I'm grateful for the gifts and the thoughtfulness behind them, it was a bit of a bummer not to see more tick marks off my wish list. Nevertheless, I'm determined to make the best of what I received.

In the spirit of the season, I'll make it work. Maybe there's a way these gifts will come in handy or brighten someone else's day if I decide to pass them along. Here's to finding joy in unexpected surprises!

Merry Christmas!

Jane

-x-X-x-X-x-X-x-X-x-X-x-X-x-X-x-

December 27th

Dear Diary,

This afternoon I found my mom and Gigi doing a video call with Aunt Val. They were all deep in conversation, sharing updates and laughing about something or the other. It felt like ages before they were done.

At that point, I got a chance to chat with my cousin Dominique. She told me her stepmom was expecting a baby and that she got to feel it kick! We also talked about what we got for Christmas. When I brought up school, she seemed a bit distant. She mentioned that she was having a few issues with friends she used to be close with but I could tell she didn't really want to get into it. I told her she could always talk to me. She thanked me and went back to her bubbly self.

Hoping the new year is better for us both.

Jane

January

January 1st

Dear Diary,

Happy New Year! I kicked off the year with Esmé and Alejandra. The two of them hit it off immediately, which made for an epic night!

We ordered a mountain of pizza, had an endless supply of chips, and created the perfect soda and root beer float concoctions. I'm pretty sure we had enough sugar to power a small town for a week!

We went downstairs where Esmé was able to sneak into her parent's Webflix account. We dove into a scary movie that made our hearts race. I'll admit, it was genuinely terrifying, and it made sleeping a bit challenging.

Despite the movie-induced jitters, the best part of the night was our girl talk. We chatted about everything, from school to crushes, and that's when Alejandra dropped a bombshell— she confessed she has a crush on Benji!

On the one hand, I understand. He is the cutest boy in school, and I also never told her I had a crush on him. On the other hand, I liked him first and if anybody should date him, it's me! I'm going to have to tell Alejandra I liked him first. I just need to be brave.

The clock ticked down and before I knew it, it was time to ring in the new year. Instead of the typical countdown and fireworks, my friends and I decided to do something wild—we formed an impromptu band right there on the street, armed with nothing but pots, pans, and a heap of enthusiasm.

It was pure madness, banging away on those makeshift drums and clanging the pots together in a chaotic rhythm. The other people out lighting fireworks probably thought we'd lost our minds, but honestly, we were having the time of our lives. It might have been a bit crazy, but man, was it an exhilarating way to start the year!

We went back inside and told each other our New Year's resolutions. Esmé resolved to keep her room clean, (which might be impossible...), and Alejandra resolved to go out with Benji! That totally threw me off. When it was my turn, I ended up saying something along the lines of getting good grades, but really diary, I want to make an impact at East Oak Middle School.

Ready to face the new year!

Jane

-x-X-x-X-x-X-x-X-x-X-x-X-x-X-x-

January 5th

Dear Diary,

Today was the first day back at school after winter break. It was so hard to wake up early after the last few weeks of sleeping in but I managed to get out the door on time. Once I got to school, I saw Harold at our locker. I couldn't believe how tan he was! He told me his parents had surprised him with a week- long trip to Hawaii. I was so jealous!

In homeroom, the teacher gave us our new class schedules for the second semester. All of my core classes are the same but I have new electives. I'm taking an art class, and of course, P.E. I'm excited for art class because I hear the teacher is super cool and at the end of the semester, we're going to make these amazing 3-D masks. I hope the rumors are true!

Even though it was the first day back we had a robotics practice, and guess what? Benji and I ended up having a blast together! It was one of those days where the usual tension melted away, and we just clicked. We joked around and laughed at the silliest things. Gia kept giving us annoyed looks because we were goofing off too much, but it didn't stop us.

I've always wanted to connect with Benji beyond robotics and today felt like a breakthrough. I'm excited about the prospect of a friendship blossoming... and maybe more.

Ready to tackle the new school year!

Jane

-x-X-x-X-x-X-x-X-x-X-x-X-x-X-x-

January 7th

Dear Diary,

The robotics team has started to meet twice a week in preparation for the competition. Gia assigned me to manage the team website. At first, I wasn't sure about it, but I've found that designing the website is surprisingly exciting—I've been adding pictures, creating our team profile, and making it look as sleek as possible.

I'm feeling really good about the website as well as the robot! I think we might win this thing!

Your extraordinary website designer!

Jane

-x-X-x-X-x-X-x-X-x-X-x-X-x-X-x-

January 11th

Dear Diary,

Guess what? It's a snow day! The world outside is covered in a thick layer of snow, and the entire neighborhood looks like a winter wonderland.

I started the day by going to the backyard with my dad and brothers. Joey and Carl's enthusiasm for the snow quickly turned into a full-on snowball fight! It was me and Dad against the boys. I have to say, having Dad on my side was an unfair advantage! Dad is a snowball-throwing machine! Luckily my brothers didn't seem to care that they were getting pummeled.

After building a very lopsided snowman, we went inside to warm up. Dad made us some hot chocolate. We used some leftover candy canes to stir the marshmallows around. As the candy canes disintegrated, we ended up with an amazing peppermint/chocolate treat!

I feel so happy that I got a chance to spend time with my dad and brothers. Hopefully, we can have a few more snow days this year.

Fingers crossed!

Jane

-x-X-x-X-x-X-x-X-x-X-x-X-x-X-x-

January 12th

Dear Diary,

It's the day after the snow day, and things are back to normal. We are only a few days away from the robotics competition, and the entire team is on edge.

Today's practice today was intense! Everyone seemed to be working tirelessly to fine-tune our robot and polish our strategies. It's like the competition has turned our normally fun-filled practices into a pressure cooker.

I also was meticulously working on the team website. With so much changing in the last few days, I feel like I've had to redo it at least 10 times! I just hope we can pull everything together for the competition.

Hoping we can get it together in time!

Jane

-x-X-x-X-x-X-x-X-x-X-x-X-x-X-x-

January 15th

Dear Diary,

Today's robotics competition was an exhilarating ride! I had to wake up at six in the morning so mom could get me to the college where the competition was being held. I felt like a zombie until we got there. Then, the excitement of the competition environment woke me up better than 100 cups of coffee could have! I met up with the team and we were surprised with muffins and juice from our coach.

We did our first run-through, and everything seemed to go haywire! For some reason, the robot was turning to the right which caused it to miss every single mission. We pulled out the laptops and reworked our code until the robot finally worked.

Despite the initial setbacks, we pushed through. Our second and third attempts were a different story altogether! The robot executed the missions flawlessly and surpassed our expectations. The rush of adrenaline and relief that surged through us with each successful mission was unbeatable!

At the closing ceremony, when the final results were announced, we couldn't believe it! Second place! Even though I joined robotics to be closer to Benji, I do feel like it's something I love to do.

Cheers to the robotics team!

Jane

January 17th

Dear Diary,

At lunch today Alejandra started flirting with Benji! She kept saying she was so proud of him for getting second place in the robotics competition. Harold and I were sitting there too, and even though we were part of the team, we didn't hear a single "Good job" or "Way to go".

Benji seemed uneasy. He kept glancing over to the table where the popular kids sat. I couldn't help but wonder if he was planning to sit with them to escape Alejandra's flirting. In the end, though, he stuck it out.

I need to have a heart-to-heart with Alejandra and tell her about my feelings for Benji. I don't want this whole crush thing to come between us or make things awkward.

Feeling like a chicken.

Jane

January 19th

Dear Diary,

I can't believe I still haven't talked to Alejandra! This is totally ridiculous! She is one of my best friends at school so I should be able to tell her anything, right?

I have got to do this soon!

Jane

-x-X-x-X-x-X-x-X-x-X-x-X-x-X-x-

January 21st

Dear Diary,

So, you know how I wanted to talk to Alejandra about us both having a crush on Benji? It turns out I don't have to have that conversation because something else happened.

<u>BENJI AND *JANEY* STARTED GOING OUT!</u>

Not only am I devastated by this news, but Alejandra is mad, and Harold has been super mopey. How is it that my best friend group is so affected by this news? I know I should still talk with Alejandra about our shared crush, but it doesn't make sense to complicate an already complicated situation.

Alejandra has declared "war" on *Janey*. I'm not exactly sure what this means, but I can tell she won't give up her crush on Benji without a fight. Now that I think about it, maybe it's best I didn't tell her about my crush. Seeing the way she's acting, I'm not sure our friendship could survive us liking the same boy.

Preparing for battle.

Jane

-x-X-x-X-x-X-x-X-x-X-x-X-x-X-x-

January 24th

Dear Diary,

I honestly thought Alejandra would have used the weekend to cool down about the whole Benji/*Janey* situation, but boy was I wrong. She had spent the weekend making a diabolical plan to break them up before Valentine's Day. I really don't know if I should be impressed or worried.

After school, she pulled me aside and told me her plan: She spent the weekend making anonymous love letters. Over the next week, she will put the letters in *Janey's* locker. Then she will start a rumor about how Benji is seeing a girl from another school. For the final piece of the plan, Alejandra is going to sneak some lip-gloss, scrunchies, and a love note into his backpack. When *Janey* sees/hears about these mysterious items, she will break up with him and want to go out with her secret admirer.

I've been fighting an internal battle ever since she told me her plan. On one hand, it would be good for them to break up, because I'd also like a chance to date Benji. But going out of her way to ruin the relationship feels wrong!

Help! I don't know what to do!

Jane

January 27th

Dear Diary,

As usual, I have been too nervous and shy to tell Alejandra I don't like her plan. I thought that maybe by staying quiet, I could stay out of the drama, but it doesn't seem like she will let me off that easily.

Yesterday at lunch, we overheard some of the popular kids ask *Janey* about the notes she's been getting. She confirmed that she had been getting anonymous love notes, but it's super annoying because she is with Benji.

On top of that, someone saw Alejandra slipping the note into *Janey*'s locker! Talk about a close call! Luckily, Alejandra was wearing the school hoodie (which half of the students own), and her identity was hidden.

What's worse than the drama is how negative Alejandra has become. All she wants to do is talk bad about *Janey*. Even though that girl annoys me, I think my friend is going a little too far.

Losing my mind!

Jane

-x-X-x-X-x-X-x-X-x-X-x-X-x-X-x-

January 28th

Dear Diary,

Today I reached my limit with Alejandra. When I got to school, she ushered me over to her locker and handed me some scrunchies, a pink notebook, lip gloss, and a charm bracelet. I was super confused. Were they gifts? No.

Alejandra asked if I could slip the items into Benji's backpack since we sit close to each other in science class. I couldn't believe it! She wants me to do the dirty work for her and in such a busy class. To avoid confronting Alejandra, I put the items in my backpack and went about my day.

Harold could tell that I was feeling off. When we were at our locker, he asked me what was going on. That's when I broke down and told him everything! I didn't mean to, but it all just came out.

After I explained Alejandra's plan, he was quiet for a minute. I could tell that he had 1000 thoughts racing in his mind. When he finally spoke, he said that we needed to put a stop to her plan, and I agreed.

At lunch we confronted Alejandra. Harold started by telling her that he knew about the plan. She got really mad at me for telling him, but Harold jumped in and defended me. He told Alejandra that it wasn't my fault. She never should've come up with a plan to break up Benji and Janey, let alone act on it.

I felt so bad because Alejandra began to tear up right in the middle of the lunchroom. She said that we don't understand how heartbreaking it is to see the person you like go out with someone else.

Harold told her that he does understand because he likes *Janey*. He confessed his feelings just like that! He also said that Benji and *Janey* had to decide for themselves if they wanted to be together. Nobody else has the right to make that choice. Honestly, you'd never know Harold was so wise by looking at him.

Alejandra agreed to stop her mission if we both promised to not tell anybody the secret admirer notes were from her. We agreed. She also apologized to both of us for acting so crazy the past few days.

Done with the drama.

Jane

February

February 1st

Dear Diary,

Today, I video chatted with my cousin Dominique, and boy, did she have some news. She started dating a boy named Grayson! She's expecting all sorts of sweet treats from him on Valentine's Day, and she's thrilled because it's her first Valentine's Day with a boyfriend.

As happy as I am for her, I can't help feeling a twinge of jealousy. Especially now that my crush is dating someone else.

Until then, I'll be cheering Dominique on from the sidelines and hoping she has a wonderful first Valentine's Day with her boyfriend.

Looking for love,

Jane

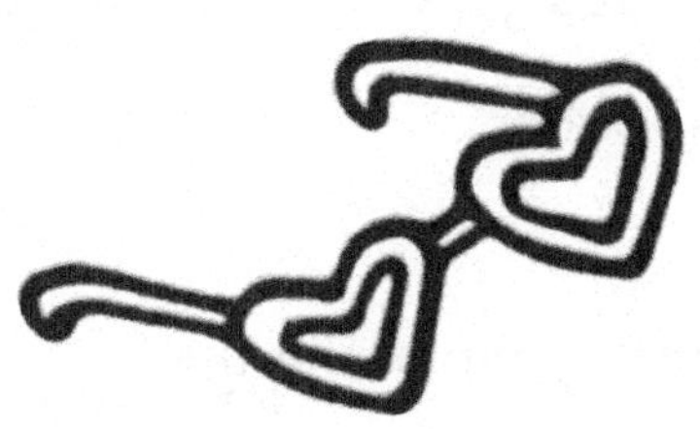

February 4th

Dear Diary,

I've been in a funk the last few days. Every day seems like a copy of the one before. School, lunch, more school, and then back home for homework—rinse and repeat. I'm slowly going nuts with the monotony!

It's not that I don't enjoy hanging out with Harold, and Alejandra, but lately, something feels off. I guess I'm just tired of the same routine, the same conversations, and the same homework. There's this itch for something different, something more exciting, but I don't know what that would be.

Anyway, I'm hoping to shake off this feeling soon. It's just been a bit tough getting through these days.

Ready for a change.

Jane

February 7th

Dear Diary,

Valentine's Day is nearly here, and our school has something exciting planned! The student council is gearing up to sell these adorable pink carnations next week, and it's got everyone buzzing. But here's the best part: when you buy one, they give you a note to fill out for whoever you're sending the flower to. Then, the student council takes charge and will deliver the flowers on Valentine's Day.

I'm going to surprise Harold and Alejandra with some carnations. They're the best friends a girl could ask for, and I want to show them how much they mean to me. Who knows, maybe I'll send some flowers to my friends on the robotics team...

Diary, I know what I'm about to admit is a bit silly, but I really, really hope someone will buy carnations for me. It would be amazing to feel that special flutter in my heart as the student council kids give me a handful of pink flowers. I mean, who wouldn't want a sweet surprise on Valentine's Day?

I've been imagining how lovely it will be to walk into school on Valentine's Day. The halls of East Oak will be filled with laughter, love, and friends surprising each other—it sounds like a scene from a movie!

Ready for a beautiful bouquet...

Jane

-x-X-x-X-x-X-x-X-x-X-x-X-x-X-x-

February 10th

Dear Diary,

Today I bought pink carnations for Harold and Alejandra, just like I planned. They're both going to be so surprised when Monday comes around. Mission accomplished!

I also did something unexpected and totally nerve-wracking. I bought an extra carnation. Not for Harold or Alejandra, but for Benji.

I know—I can't believe I did it either! I was standing in line, and before I knew it, I'd picked up an extra flower and paid for it. But here's the catch: he's still dating *Janey.*

Look diary, in no way am I trying to cause a problem for their relationship. I just really like him and I have to express myself. In the end, I left the notecard blank.

Fingers crossed for some Valentine's magic,

Jane

-x-X-x-X-x-X-x-X-x-X-x-X-x-X-x-

Valentine's Day, February 14th

Dear Diary,

Today was... well, it was something else. Valentine's Day arrived, and with it came a flurry of pink and red. Our classrooms turned into a floral paradise when the student council members burst in, handing out carnations to everyone.

Happy Valentines Day

Harold and Alejandra surprised me with a carnation each, just like the ones I'd given them. It was so sweet, and I couldn't help but feel all warm and fuzzy inside. But hold on, here's the crazy twist of the day: Harold ended up getting a couple more flowers from Gia! I saw him reading the note, and wow, did he turn red like a tomato!

I had my next class with Benji who ended up getting a whole bouquet of carnations! My heart sank a little when I saw that.

I didn't put my name on the card attached to my carnation, thinking it would be less awkward that way, but now I'm kind of regretting it. He got so many flowers; mine probably didn't stand out at all! Maybe next time I'll muster up the courage to write my name. Despite all that, it was a nice day.

Feeling the love,

Jane

-x-X-x-X-x-X-x-X-x-X-x-X-x-X-x-

February 17th

Dear Diary,

My birthday is just around the corner! I've been wanting a cell phone so earlier tonight I asked Mom and Dad for one. I told them that's all I want for my birthday, and I'm serious! I wouldn't need anything else if I just got a phone.

Their reaction wasn't what I hoped for. They didn't say yes, but they didn't say no either. It was more like a hesitant "We'll think about it". Ugh, why does it have to be so complicated?

I get it, having a phone comes with responsibilities, and they're worried about me spending too much time on it. But I promised them I'd be responsible and follow their rules! I just want to feel a bit more independent, especially now that I'm getting older.

I'm really hoping they'll surprise me on my birthday with that shiny new phone. I've even started researching different models and imagining all the cool things I could do with it.

Ready for some tech!

Jane

February 21st

Dear Diary,

Today was the best birthday ever! It felt like the universe conspired to make it extra special. It started with my favorite breakfast made by Mom—waffles with chocolate chips. When my brothers came into the kitchen, they both greeted me with birthday hugs and kisses. It was a pleasant surprise.

And then, at school, Harold and Alejandra nailed it with their gifts. I got an adorable half-heart friendship necklace from Alejandra and the next book in my favorite series from Harold! Even the teachers seemed to be in on the birthday magic. No homework and an overall chill vibe in my classes.

But wait, it gets even better!

When I got home, the day hit its peak. We had spaghetti for dinner, and then came the moment I was waiting for—gift time! And guess what?

Among all the wonderful presents, there it was—a brand-new cell phone!

I couldn't believe it! It was like a dream come true. Sure, it has parental controls, but I expected that. I spent the whole evening setting it up, personalizing it, and exploring all its features. I might have gone a little overboard with the emojis, but who can blame me? I'm beyond thrilled!

My parents made my birthday special, and I'm grateful for their thoughtful gift, even with the restrictions. This day was pure magic, and I'm feeling incredibly lucky and loved.

Cheers to year twelve!

Jane

-x-X-x-X-x-X-x-X-x-X-x-X-x-X-x-

February 22nd

Dear Diary,

Okay, so yesterday was epic, but today? Today is a whole new level of awesome! I got to show off my new phone to Harold and Alejandra. They were so excited for me, and we exchanged numbers right away.

Before school even started, we were already texting each other the funniest things. It felt like this whole new world had opened up—I mean, who knew texting could be so much fun? (Apparently everybody.)

After school, I was able to get Esmé and Dominique's phone numbers from my mom. It feels so great to be able to chat with my friends whenever I want, and not have to wait for my mom to give me her phone.

I can't wait to explore more of what this phone can do: emojis, GIFs, music, photography, and all those cool apps! But for now, I'm just reveling in the joy of communication with the people I love.

Here's to the start of something wonderful,

Jane

-x-X-x-X-x-X-x-X-x-X-x-X-x-X-x-

February 24th

Dear Diary,

When I was walking home from school today my neighbor, Mrs. Brookshire, asked if I wanted to babysit her two daughters, Gemma and Louisa. I was super excited about it! I ran home and mentioned it to Mom, but she threw me a curveball—I have to practice by babysitting Joey and Carl tomorrow night.

I get it, I do. Mom wants to make sure I can handle it, but my brothers are a handful! They're way more mischievous and rambunctious than Gemma and Louisa.

I agreed to Mom's terms because I really want to prove that I can be a babysitter. But now, I'm not so sure if it was the best idea. What if my brothers decide to pull off a crazy stunt while Mom and Dad are out? What if I can't handle them and end up ruining my chance to babysit?

I've been trying to think positive thoughts and come up with a plan to keep my brothers entertained and out of trouble. I just hope everything goes smoothly and that I can prove I'm responsible enough for this babysitting gig.

Hoping for a chaos-free evening,

Jane

February 25th

Dear Diary,

Tonight was a babysitting adventure! Watching my brothers turned out to be way more challenging than I expected, but I managed to keep control.

As soon as mom and dad left my brothers started bouncing off the walls. It was pure chaos! I was starting to worry that I wouldn't be able to handle them, especially when they refused to listen to me.

But then, I had a stroke of genius! I suggested we turn cleaning up into a game— a relay race through the house. It was like magic! They got super excited about racing each other to pick up their toys, and before we knew it, the toy room was all tidy. It was both fun and productive!

After that, we settled down for a movie with popcorn. It was a peaceful end to what started as a wild evening. They were completely engrossed, and I finally got a chance to catch my breath.

When Mom and Dad came home, they were surprised to find everything in order and my brothers happily watching the movie. Dad said he was proud of how I managed the whole evening! Hearing that made me feel really good. And the best part? Mom said I did such a great job that I'm ready to babysit Gemma and Louisa!

I am so ready for my first babysitting gig.

Jane

-x-X-x-X-x-X-x-X-x-X-x-X-x-X-x-

February 27th

Dear Diary,

Babysitting Gemma and Louisa was a breeze compared to my brothers! They're so much gentler and easier to manage. It was an awesome experience from start to finish.

We had a blast playing fairies for a few hours. They had the most vivid imaginations, and it was amazing to see how creative they could be. Then we switched to coloring, which was a calming and fun activity.

When it was lunchtime, I whipped up some peanut butter and jelly sandwiches, and they loved it! It felt great to make something they enjoyed, and I was glad they liked the simple meal.

But the best part? After three hours of babysitting, I got paid $45! I couldn't believe it! I mean, it was so much fun hanging out with Gemma and Louisa, and getting paid for it was the cherry on top. Babysitting was a blast, and I can't wait for my next babysitting job.

Your babysitter extraordinaire,

Jane

March

March 3rd

Dear Diary,

East Oak Middle School is gearing up for an epic staff versus student dodgeball game the day before spring break. It's the talk of the town, or at least the talk of the school halls!

Okay, so brace yourself for this news: I got asked to team up with the robotics team! And let me tell you, if anyone thinks they're just "nerdy" kids, they couldn't be more wrong. People like Benji and Gia, are into robotics and sports! How cool is that?

Even though Alejandra wasn't on the robotics team, she was asked to fill in one of the last two spots. She was flattered but declined the invitation saying it wasn't her thing. The only downside to the team lineup? Benji invited *Janey* to join. It's a bit annoying, but I guess I'll make the best of it.

I'm beyond excited and just a tad nervous. This is my chance to make an impression and to show Benji that I'm not just a girl who anonymously gave him a Valentine's Day carnation. I want to prove that I'm fun, cool, and dodgeball-ready.

After school, I convinced my brothers to throw beachballs at me so I can practice my dodging! I'm determined to be a great player and, hopefully, catch Benji's eye in a good way. Who knows, maybe after I show off my skills, he'll realize I'm the girl for him and break up with Janey.

I'm counting down the days until the big game. It's going to be legendary, and who knows, maybe it'll be the start of something... well, something great.

Darting, diving, and dodging!

Jane

March 8th

Dear Diary,

The dodgeball team made a group chat through text, and let me tell you—it's the absolute best! Suddenly, I'm texting with a whole bunch of people, and it feels like we're forming this tight-knit group. It's amazing how a few texts can make you feel so much closer to others.

And guess who's standing out in the chat? Harold! He's chill in person, but in the group chat, he's cracking the best jokes. His texts make me laugh so hard. I'm not the only one finding him hilarious, Gia hearts every funny picture and comment he sends.

Between the jokes we've been planning for our big game, and the latest decision? Dressing up in neon colors! We're going to be so eye-catching, and I can't wait to see everyone glowing on the court.

There's something about these group chats that makes me feel like I belong, like I'm part of a cool squad. I'm genuinely excited about the game, but I'm even more excited about this growing bond with everyone on the team. It's like we're building something awesome, and it feels amazing.

To neon colors and newfound friendships,

Jane

-x-X-x-X-x-X-x-X-x-X-x-X-x-X-x-

March 12th

Dear Diary,

Mom and I went shopping for a neon pink shirt. I found the cutest tank top that screams "neon" from miles away. It's so bright, I might just light up the entire gym all on my own!

But that's not all—I also stumbled upon these amazing bright purple leggings that go perfectly with the tank top. I feel like I've transformed into a walking neon sign, and I'm loving it! It's like the colors are radiating happiness.

I'm so excited about the dodgeball game now. I can already picture our team, all decked out in these vibrant colors, ready to take on the staff. It's going to be a blast, and I can't wait to show off my neon ensemble!

Here's to feeling like a walking rainbow,

Jane

-x-X-x-X-x-X-x-X-x-X-x-X-x-X-x-

March 18th

Dear Diary,

Today was the dodgeball tournament, and it was intense! Our neon team was doing great, making our way through the rounds, and then came the semi-finals against the camo team.

It was down to the wire, and somehow, I ended up being the last player on our team against four of the toughest kids in the sixth grade. Talk about pressure! I did my best to catch those dodgeballs flying at me, but one slipped out of my hand, and that was it. Our team lost.

I could feel the disappointment radiating from my teammates, and even though they said it wasn't my fault it still stung. I felt like I let them down, especially being the last one standing. It's tough when you're the one who makes the final mistake, you know?

The only silver lining was that we avoided playing the teachers in the final round. They looked ferocious out there, taking out some serious pent-up frustration on the winning team. Phew, dodged that bullet!

Hoping for better dodgeball days ahead,

Jane

-x-X-x-X-x-X-x-X-x-X-x-X-x-X-x-

March 20th

Dear Diary,

Oh, spring break boredom is hitting hard! I thought I'd have tons of plans, but here I am, staring at the ceiling and counting the tiles. Alejandra went back to Texas to visit her mom and Harold has a jam-packed schedule with no chill time. I'm stuck with nothing to do.

I've scrolled through my phone a million times, watched way too many random videos, and attempted to start a new TV series, only to realize I'm not really in the mood for it. It's like the boredom is on a mission to drive me crazy!

I guess I could try picking up a new hobby or finding something different to do around the house, but everything feels kind of blah right now.

Fading fast...

Jane

-x-X-x-X-x-X-x-X-x-X-x-X-x-X-x-

March 22nd

Dear Diary,

You know what I've noticed? The dodgeball group chat has been strangely quiet lately, and it's kind of sad. It used to be this lively space where we'd share jokes, plan practices, and just goof around. But now, it's like someone hit the mute button. I miss those moments of laughter and connection.

Feeling a bit down, I decided to reach out to Esmé. We haven't really talked since I texted her my phone number and she wished me a happy birthday. I definitely feel guilty for neglecting our friendship...

Esmé was really happy to get my text, and after catching up we made plans to go see a movie later this week. There's something comforting about having plans to look forward to, especially during this stretch of spring break boredom.

Here's to reconnecting and growing new memories,

Jane

March 23rd

Dear Diary,

Today was a blast! Hanging out with Esmé was exactly what I needed. Our moms took us to see this hilarious cartoon cat movie, and let me tell you, we were laughing so hard our sides hurt!

After the movie, her mom treated us to lunch at this fancy Italian restaurant. I swear, I ate so much pasta I felt like I was going to turn into a noodle! It was delicious, but I definitely overdid it. Note to self: there's a limit to how much pasta a person can eat in a single sitting. After lunch, our moms took us shopping at some outlet stores. While they were busy browsing clothes, Esmé and I wandered around and ended up having a heart-to-heart.

Esmé opened up about these mean girls who've been giving her a hard time, and how she's struggling in math class. After she vented, we were able to brainstorm some ideas to help her.

Hopefully, the rest of the school year will turn out better for her.

And guess what, diary? I decided to open up about my struggles. I told her how I've been having a hard time fitting in, and how every time I make progress there seems to be a bump in the road that crushes my confidence. Esmé was amazing and gave me a lot of great advice and support.

Today reminded me how great of a friend Esmé is. I need to make sure we don't drift apart like we have been over the past few months. I'm going to make it a priority to reach out to her more often.

Here's to best friends!

Jane

March 25th

Dear Diary,

I've been doing a lot of thinking lately, and I've come to a decision—I want to reinvent myself. Coming back from spring break feels like a fresh start, a chance to finally feel like I fit in.

The first step to becoming the "new and improved" Jane is confidence. It's time to shed the constant nervousness and embrace who I truly am. It's about staying authentic to myself.

The second part (which is way more fun) is reinventing my look. I've been browsing different styles online, trying to figure out what resonates with me. It's exciting, to think about the possibilities!

Something I'm super excited about is the idea of dyeing my hair. Maybe a bold color like blue or purple—just to add a little pop to my look. I hope I can convince Mom to let me do it. It feels like the perfect way to kick off this reinvention.

There's this bubbling excitement inside me! It's like I've found a new spark that's pushing me forward. Change can be scary, but it's also exhilarating.

Time to take charge of my life!

Jane

-x-X-x-X-x-X-x-X-x-X-x-X-x-X-x-

March 27th

Dear Diary,

Today was beyond amazing! I talked to Mom about my ideas for a new style, and guess what? She was totally on board with it! She said we couldn't redo my entire wardrobe because it would be too expensive, but we could go shopping and grab a few new pieces to spice things up.

And the best part? Mom said I could get a few purple streaks in my hair! I couldn't believe it. It's like a dream come true.

We spent the day shopping and picked out clothes that felt more like "me". It was so much fun trying out different styles and experimenting with what felt right. Mom was such a trooper, giving her input and making the day super enjoyable.

You got this, Girl!

After we found the perfect clothes, we drove to the hair salon. I was a bundle of nerves and excitement at the same time. The stylist there was cool and helped me choose a shade that would suit me. It was exhilarating watching my plain hair transform with streaks of electric purple! The stylist also gave me some layers, so now my grown-out bob looks way trendier!

Today was more than just a shopping spree or a hair makeover—it was a day of bonding with Mom, making memories, and becoming 'ME'.

Ready to rock my new look!

Jane

-x-X-x-X-x-X-x-X-x-X-x-X-x-X-x-

March 28th

Dear Diary,

It felt amazing stepping into school with my new style. I was turning heads, and I got compliments left and right. Even Harold was looking at me like I was a new person!

But then, there was this weird moment. Alejandra said she didn't like the change! She mentioned that it was "too much" and that I seemed different. I won't lie, it hurt my feelings.

I guess I hadn't anticipated that not everyone would be on board with the new look. It's funny how a small comment from someone you care about can have such an impact. It kind of made me question my decision for a moment.

But then I reminded myself that this transformation wasn't about pleasing everyone else—it was about me feeling comfortable and confident in my skin. Maybe Alejandra needs some time.

The only person who didn't get a chance to see my new style was Benji. Maybe he's on an extended spring break trip with his family or something. Hopefully, he'll be back at school soon so he can check out my new look!

Confidently yours, 

Jane

-x-X-x-X-x-X-x-X-x-X-x-X-x-X-x-

March 29th

Dear Diary,

Benji made quite the entrance at school today, sporting a colossal red cast on his left arm! It was an instant attention-grabber! We all swarmed around him, eager to hear the story of how he ended up with the cast. He was a little too eager on his ski trip and wiped out. After the story, he passed around a Sharpie so we could all sign the cast.

After I signed my name, I noticed that *Janey* had written her name big, and she added a heart. She's so annoying! We all know they are boyfriend/girlfriend so she didn't need to take up that much space. Since I was one of the last people to sign, there was barely any room. I ended up signing my name really small on his elbow where he's never going to see it. I'm trying not to let it bother me, but it's hard.

For now, I'll focus on sending positive vibes for a speedy recovery and try not to overthink the small stuff.

Hoping he recovers soon!

Jane

-x-X-x-X-x-X-x-X-x-X-x-X-x-X-x-

March 30th

Dear Diary,

I got an apology from Alejandra today. She said that I do look nice with my new hair and clothes and she's sorry for being rude. I told her it hurt my feelings that one of my best friends was so quick to put me down.

We ended up having a deep conversation where she told me her reaction came from all the changes she has been through. I asked her what she meant, and she opened up about why her family moved.

One year ago, Alejandra was living her normal life in Texas. Her parents started arguing all the time, which led to their separation. While her parents were separated her mom met a new man which led to a divorce. During the divorce, her parents decided to sell the house, which led to her moving here. Now she lives in a new state, in a new house, with her sisters and dad. In her world, change leads to bad things.

I'm really happy I got an apology and that I have a better understanding of my friend's life.

All is forgiven.

Jane

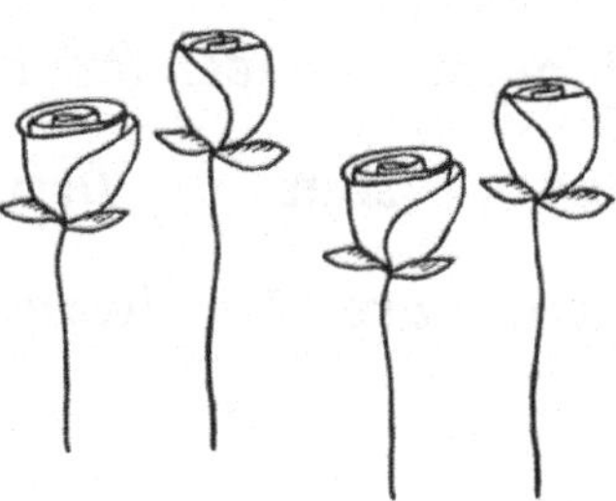

March 31st

Dear Diary,

Something unexpected happened today. I got paired up with *Janey* for a major ELA project. At first, I was a bit hesitant to work with her, but as we started brainstorming ideas, something surprising happened... *Janey* actually gave me a compliment on one of my ideas!

It was unexpected but in a good way. Before I knew it, we were bouncing ideas off each other, and there was this weird productive flow between us.

The most surprising part? We ended up exchanging phone numbers! I never would've guessed that this project would lead to me texting my rival all night. I guess it's a reminder that first impressions aren't always

accurate and that sometimes, the people you least expect can surprise you.

Here's to breaking down rivalries,

Jane

April

April 2nd

Dear Diary,

Another babysitting success! I spent the afternoon watching Gemma and Louisa. We had a great time playing an adventure game, plus getting paid $30 for hanging out with them is a pretty sweet deal!

But wait, there's more! April 17th is Mrs. Brookshire's birthday. She's having some people over for a small party and she wanted to know if I'd be willing to watch Gemma, Louisa, and their cousins while she and her friends hung out upstairs. I eagerly agreed—I mean, why wouldn't I?

I'm excited about this upcoming babysitting gig. It's nice to know how much they trust me!

Business is booming!

Jane

April 4th

Dear Diary,

Today took an unexpected turn. Benji and Janey got into this heated argument in the hallway, and it was tense, to say the least.

It's kind of hard to explain, but seeing them clash left me feeling a mix of emotions. On one hand, I felt really bad about it because nobody likes to see conflict. But then, there's this other side, this tiny part of me that sees it as a chance—an opportunity to step in and get Benji's attention.

Knowing that there is a possibility of them breaking up, makes me think I should finally get around to telling Alejandra about my crush on Benji...

It's a tricky situation,

Jane

April 5th

Dear Diary,

IT'S OFFICIAL!

<u>BENJI AND *JANEY* BROKE UP!</u>

On one hand, I am sad for Benji and *Janey*. Both of them are going through a hard time and dealing with heartbreak. On the other hand, if they weren't getting along the breakup might be for the best. I just think people should be with someone they get along with. A good relationship wouldn't have you screaming at each other in the school's halls, right?

In ELA class, I told *Janey* I was sorry to hear that they broke up. I could tell she appreciated my words, but she still seemed kind of down. When the teacher gave us time to work on our project, I made a lot of goofy jokes. For a little bit, she seemed to forget about her heartache and just laughed.

Hoping the heartbreak heals.

Jane

April 8th

Dear Diary,

Working on this ELA project with Janey has been quite an experience! We've been at it for a week now, and the deadline is looming—only three school days left.

Janey invited me to sit with her at lunch so we could do some impromptu work, much to the annoyance of Alejandra and Harold (I'm actually not sure if Harold is annoyed, or if he's jealous I'm spending time with his crush).

Diary, I do have a bit of a confession: even though Janey and I have been spending our lunches together to get work done, we've barely talked about the project! It's like we're friends first and project partners second.

It's strange how spending time with someone you once saw as a rival can change things. Who knew that a project could lead to unexpected bonding? But hey, maybe this is how friendships start—through shared experiences.

Making a fast friend!

Jane

April 13th

Dear Diary,

We did it! The ELA project is finally finished, and I couldn't be prouder! We made a book trailer that turned out amazing, and even the teacher said it was one of the best he'd ever seen! It feels incredible to receive such positive feedback, especially after all the hard work Janey and I put into it.

In a moment of pure excitement, Janey asked if we should celebrate after school. I couldn't resist that idea. I texted Mom, and she agreed that I could go with Janey and her mom to get frozen yogurt after school. It's a little surreal how things have changed. We went from being rivals (in my mind) to celebrating our project together.

Here's to newfound friendships,

Jane

April 16th

Dear Diary,

Today was my brother Carl's birthday celebration. We went to this huge arcade that had everything from go-karts to a tilt-a- whirl. Oh man, that ride was something else!

I rode it way too many times and almost ended up losing my lunch. After that, I stuck to the arcade for the rest of the day.

It was also nice to spend time with my older cousins, Rebecca and Noah. I hadn't seen them since Christmas. We shared stories, laughed endlessly, and I couldn't resist telling them about my newfound friendship with Janey.

But then, the mood shifted when my cousin Noah made this comment about how Janey would finally make me popular. It caught me off guard. I explained to Noah that sixth grade has been about finding where I belong. It's never been about popularity. Janey and I genuinely clicked in a way that feels so real. He seemed to get it after I said it like that.

It hasn't been an easy journey, but I finally feel like I'm growing into the person I'm meant to be.

Finally finding my voice.

Jane

-x-X-x-X-x-X-x-X-x-X-x-X-x-X-x-

April 17th

Dear Diary,

Today was my babysitting gig. Gemma and Louisa were beyond excited to hang out with their cousins, Arthur and Carmen. Let me tell you, things got chaotic fast!

Keeping up with the kid's antics was a challenge, but somehow, we made it through those three hours. We played on the swing set in their backyard. Then, I managed to have them compete in a relay race I set up. At times, it felt like four tornadoes were spinning around the room, but I managed to keep control while having some fun too.

In the end, I made $90 from the gig, and I'm pretty proud of myself for handling the chaos. It's amazing how much energy those little ones have!

Ready to drop!

Jane

April 18th

Dear Diary,

This week is state testing. Instead of going about my regular schedule, I spent the first three hours in my homeroom class. We worked on part one of the math test. I felt confident about my answers, but here's the kicker: I finished earlier than everyone else.

I focused on my silent reading book, but I finished that pretty quickly. I ended up sitting around for what felt like an eternity while everyone else was still finishing their test. It was a bit frustrating, to be honest.

I hope the rest of the testing days don't end with me twiddling my thumbs. Fingers crossed for a more engaging experience tomorrow!

I can't wait for this week to be over!

Jane

April 21st

Dear Diary,

The last day of testing turned out to be unexpectedly amazing! I found the perfect way to pass the time while waiting for everyone to finish. Janey and I decided to write stories together—two stories actually!

We each started a story in our notebook. After we wrote a page, we switched notebooks and would continue with the other story. It's like this awesome collaboration where our imaginations ran wild!

One story was about a princess who had to learn about her magical powers and fight an evil queen trying to take her throne. The other story revolved around a girl who was sent to boarding school and had to figure out her new life there. It's incredible how our creativity just flowed.

I'm going to miss these storytelling sessions but hey, at least it's shown me how fun and writing can be.

Maybe I'll be a writer in the future!

Jane

-x-X-x-X-x-X-x-X-x-X-x-X-x-X-x-

April 22nd

Dear Diary,

During lunch today, Alejandra and Harold pulled me aside. They told me how they've been feeling a bit neglected since I've been spending so much time with Janey. Their words really got to me—I felt awful!

I explained to them that Janey and I connected during our ELA project, and the story-building stemmed from our downtime during testing. I told them I wasn't excluding them on purpose and reassured them that their friendship means the world to me.

I got so wrapped up with Janey and our stories that I didn't think about how it was coming off to my other friends. I promised to be better at balancing my time.

Hoping the three musketeers have room for one more.

Jane

-x-X-x-X-x-X-x-X-x-X-x-X-x-X-x-

April 25th

Dear Diary,

Benji got his cast removed! It's funny how it became such a big part of how I pictured him, so seeing him without it felt a bit strange.

This big change with Benji made me realize it was time to talk with Alejandra and Janey. I've hidden my feelings for Benji for too long, and I don't want to keep secrets from my friends anymore.

I had Alejandra and Janey meet at my locker after school. After Harold left, I opened up to them about having a crush on Benji throughout the year, and my worry that telling them would destroy our friendship. I said if either of them had a problem I would stop liking him right then and there!

But you know what? Alejandra and Janey just burst out laughing. Turns out, Alejandra hasn't liked Benji for the past month! Her focus has shifted to a guy named Josh in her youth group. Janey was also cool with it. She said Benji was a nice guy, but the two of them were not compatible. If I ever started dating him, she would support me and wish me luck.

Feeling 1000 pounds lighter!

Jane

April 29th

Dear Diary,

I feel horrible because I forgot about Esmé's birthday! Two whole days passed before I realized, and it left me feeling like a terrible friend.

I called her after school and told her I was sorry for forgetting. Then, after checking it was okay with my mom, I invited her to go shopping this weekend. I want to use some of the money I've earned from babysitting to get her a nice gift. It feels like the least I can do to make up for forgetting such an important day.

It's important to show my friends how much they mean to me, especially the friends I don't see at school every day. I realize I'm going to have to put in more effort.

Hoping to redeem myself.

Jane

April 30th

Dear Diary,

Mom and I went to the mall and met up with Esmé and her mom. To my surprise, our moms decided we could roam around on our own! Having that independence was exactly what we needed. It was a chance to reconnect and have some one-on-one time.

Being alone with Esmé gave me a chance to address the elephant in the room—I apologized to her for forgetting her birthday. She said that she wasn't even upset, which shocked me! She explained that what mattered to her was that I made plans to make her feel special.

When it came to picking out a gift for Esmé's birthday, I wanted it to be special. I got her this adorable headband that had fake pearls all over it, a couple of necklaces that she loved, and a shirt with a cool anime character. We even shared a giant birthday cookie from Cookie-Palooza.

I couldn't resist grabbing a few things for myself too. I found a couple of cute shirts, some stylish hair clips, and the highlight of my shopping spree—a nice pair of tennis shoes. They're super white with this cool purple emblem, and I can't wait to show them off at school.

Here's to the birthday girl!

Jane

May

May 3rd

Dear Diary,

Something really cool happened today! My rival-turned-friend, Janey, joined me at lunch. It might not seem like a big deal to some, but for me, it was kind of a moment.

Janey didn't even sit at our table when she dated Benji. Alejandra and Harold seemed happy to have her join us, and Benji didn't seem to care at all. It looks like they can be friends after the break up.

We chatted about random things, shared laughs, and before we knew it, everyone was getting along. Alejandra seemed to connect with Janey today, and seeing that bond form was just... it was kind of special, you know?

Harold, on the other hand, barely made it through his lunch. He was too busy staring at Janey with these big puppy eyes and a goofy grin.

I'm honestly not sure how Janey didn't notice his totally obvious crush!

Despite that, it's moments like these that make me appreciate how friendships can grow and mesh together, creating something unique and wonderful.

Finally fitting in with friends!

Jane

-x-X-x-X-x-X-x-X-x-X-x-X-x-X-x-

May 6th

Dear Diary,

Can you believe this heat in early May?

It feels like summer snuck in early! But hey, I'm not complaining because Harold came up with the best idea. He invited our friend group over to his house this weekend to swim in their pool. How awesome is that?

I'm so excited to hang out with everyone in this new friend group. I also can't wait to show off some of my swimming moves. It'll be great to relax and have a blast with my friends in such a cool setting.

Ready to dive into the weekend!

Jane

-x-X-x-X-x-X-x-X-x-X-x-X-x-X-x-

May 8th

Dear Diary,

Harold's pool party was a blast! Alejandra, Janey, and I showed up at his house around noon and were surprised with a ton of Chinese food. Let me tell you, it was delicious! But when it was time to hit the water, I started feeling a bit off. It could have been nerves or too many egg rolls, who knows?

I took a quick breather by the poolside, trying to shake off the jitters. Eventually, I decided to literally dive in and let loose. The moment I hit the water all the worries disappeared. I showed off some of my diving skills, which was so much fun! It felt great to twist and turn mid-air before splashing into the pool.

We also raced, and guess what? I ended up beating everyone! It was awesome swimming with my friends, but I could sense my competitive spirit coming out. I made sure to tell everyone "Good job," and not be a sore winner.

However, there was this one thing that kind of got to me—I was the only girl not in a bikini. I wore my trusty swimsuit from my time on the swim team. It didn't bother me much, but it felt a tad awkward. I mean, everyone looked cool in their bikinis, and there I was, in my regular swim gear.

Anyway, aside from that, it was a fabulous day filled with laughter, games and some good ol' pool fun.

Exhausted and ready for a nap.

Jane

May 9th

Dear Diary,

At lunch, we were buzzing about our weekend at Harold's house. We chatted about the Chinese food feast and all the fun we had, and then, out of nowhere Benji joined our conversation! He asked about our weekend, and I couldn't help but share how awesome it was.

And here's the cool part—Harold invited Benji to the next pool party! Benji seems genuinely excited to be invited and agreed to go next time. Having Benji join us will make the next pool day even more epic. I'm looking forward to hanging out with the gang again and having Benji there will just add to the fun.

Here's to hoping the hot weather will last forever!

Jane

May 13th

Dear Diary,

Well, the weather took a complete turn! It's suddenly gotten cold, which means no chance for another pool party this weekend. I was really looking forward to some more swimming fun, especially with Benji planning on joining us. Guess I'll have to wait a bit longer for another pool day.

But hey, on a brighter note, our school just announced there's going to be a talent show! I've been thinking about it since they mentioned it. It sounds like an amazing opportunity, and I'm psyched about the idea of showcasing some talent. I wonder what everyone else is planning to do.

Time to tackle a new talent!

Jane

May 16th

Dear Diary,

Today, Harold, Alejandra, Janey, and I were talking about the talent show during lunch. After a bit of discussion, we decided we should perform!

Janey brought up the cutie-bear incident. She said it was an amazing performance until the unfortunate "underwear incident". Alejandra looked utterly confused, so I told her the story of what had happened, and guess what, we all laughed about it! Even me!

After we had a good laugh, we decided to each come up with a list of songs that would be fun to perform to. I'm also going to ask Mom and Dad if we can practice at my house after school, kind of like what Harold and did for the Halloween dance.

Here's to a dance redo!

Jane

May 20th

Dear Diary,

After a week of practice, we've finally nailed down the song and basic moves to our dance! Our routine is set to this cool electronic pop song called "Instrumental Whoop" by DJ Red Barn. The rhythm is so catchy; it's the perfect track to groove to. The energy of the song matches the vibe we're going for in our routine.

We've been working on syncing our moves with the music and getting the choreography just right. It's like this electrifying feeling when we're all dancing in sync with the song—it's starting to look and feel amazing.

With each practice session, we're getting closer to creating something spectacular for the talent show. I can't wait for everyone to see!

Your superstar performer!

Jane

May 22nd

Dear Diary,

Do you remember how at the beginning of the year I wasn't doing so well in social studies? Well... my grade has dropped to a D. I thought I'd be able to get it up before my parents found out, but my dad saw it when he was checking the online grade portal, and needless to say, he wasn't thrilled. My parents made it clear that I needed to bring that grade up before friends could come over for dance practice.

I'm not going to lie, I had a major meltdown. It's just that my friends and I have been working so hard and I don't want us to lose any progress we've made. My behavior did not impress Mom, and she ended up taking my phone for a week!

I understand where she's coming from. It's so close to the end of the year, so schoolwork needs to be a priority. At the same time, why does she have to punish my friends?

I'm planning on going in tomorrow morning and talking to my teacher. Hopefully, it won't take me long to get my grade back to a B.

Hating history!

Jane

-x-X-x-X-x-X-x-X-x-X-x-X-x-X-x-

May 23rd

Dear Diary,

My social studies teacher offered a way to raise my grade: I have to give a two-minute speech about irrigation in Mesopotamia this Friday. Honestly, the topic sounds about as thrilling as watching paint dry, but I can't let this opportunity slip by, especially if it means I can start practicing with my friends again.

I'm determined to get through this speech and get back on track so that we can continue our dance practice. It's going to take some effort, but I'll make it happen. Time to learn about Mesopotamian irrigation and...

Zzzzzzzzzzzz!

Jane

-x-X-x-X-x-X-x-X-x-X-x-X-x-X-x-

May 26th

Dear Diary,

Practicing my speech has become a daily ritual. I've repeated it so many times that even my brothers are starting to spout off facts about storing water and digging canals! It's both funny and a little nerve-wracking how much they've picked up.

Even though I've practiced it countless times, the nerves are kicking in. Having to deliver the speech in front of the entire class is a whole different ball game. It's like this mix of excitement and anxiety all rolled into one.

I'm trying to stay calm and remind myself that I know this speech inside out. Hopefully, once I start talking, the nerves will fade away, and I can get through it without stumbling or freezing up.

Hoping I can pull this off...

Jane

May 27th

Dear Diary,

I did it! I got through my speech, and while it might not have been the most thrilling presentation ever, it did the trick. I managed to raise my grade to a B. Now, all I have to do is stay on top of my work for the next few weeks, and I should end the year with a decent grade.

To make up for lost time, my friends and I are heading over to Harold's house to practice our routine this weekend. Remember how his basement has that awesome audio system and projector setup? It's going to take our practice sessions to a whole new level!

Time to pull out and polish my moves!

Jane

Memorial Day, May 30th

Dear Diary,

Today was such a lovely Memorial Day. We started with a family picnic at the park. The weather was just right—a touch of warmth without being too hot. Mom packed all our favorites: sandwiches, chips, and those delicious homemade cookies. Dad even brought along a Frisbee, and we had a blast tossing it around. It was nice spending some quality time together, just enjoying each other's company.

When we got back home, I had the chance to video chat with my cousin Dominique. She's beyond excited about us spending the summer together again. She's been filling up her journal with all of her sixth-grade experiences and she is excited to share.

Can't wait for some cousin time!

Jane

June

June 3rd

Dear Diary,

Our performance at the talent show was something else! We were the second act of the night and before we went on stage, Alejandra started getting panicky because it was her first time performing in front of an audience. But our team rallied around her, offering support and reassurance.

When we finally went up to perform, the energy was electric! The adrenaline rush was overwhelming but in a good way. Everything was going smoothly until, of course, a small mishap occurred—I tripped over a cord leading to the microphone during one of my moves.

Surprisingly, I don't think anyone in the audience even noticed my little misstep. We continued with the routine flawlessly, and the audience's cheers and applause at the end were incredible!

Honestly, I was glad we performed early on in the show so we could relax and watch the rest of the performances. There was this kid on a unicycle, and I couldn't help but wonder how he even discovered that talent! It was impressive to watch him balance and maneuver with such skill.

Then, there was a girl from my PE class who sang beautifully. Her voice echoed through the auditorium, captivating everyone. It was one of those performances that gave you goosebumps.

And, of course, there was a group of boys, including Benji, who did a funny dance to an old rap song. They had the entire audience eating out of the palms of their hands. It was great to see Benji having fun and being himself. That's when he's the cutest!

Here's to celebrating everyone's unique talents!

Jane

-x-X-x-X-x-X-x-X-x-X-x-X-x-X-x-

June 6th

Dear Diary,

Finals week is creeping closer, and my stress levels is definitely rising. All my classes have finals, which is completely different from elementary school. I don't know how I'm going to prepare for all of these tests!

My ELA teacher is having us memorize a poem to recite in front of the class. Since I did that Mesopotamia speech, I'm not too worried. I've got a knack for memorizing things.

Science class sounds like it'll be fun. We get to choose one of three experiments and then do it.

It's a nice change from the typical written exam, and I'm looking forward to getting hands-on with the experiments.

I am a little intimidated by the math test

though. It covers everything we've learned through the year! The saving grace is that we can use our notes, which should help a lot. I don't mean to brag, but after writing in you all year, I have become a master note-taker!

But then there's social studies... a fifty-question multiple-choice test. That seems a bit intense, especially at the end of the year. I just hope I'll remember enough to do well.

Time to do some last-minute studying!

Jane

June 8th

Dear Diary,

Today in science class, I got paired up with Benji for our final experiment. We haven't had a chance to spend a lot of time together since the robotics season ended. It was great! We hit it off like old times and joked around a lot. It's always nice when you just have fun.

As we chatted, I mentioned that I was planning on joining the swim team again, and he seemed genuinely interested. He asked a lot of questions and mentioned it could be a way to strengthen his arm after having it in a cast for so long. I hope he seriously considers joining!

Hoping for a summer with my crush!

Jane

June 10th

Dear Diary,

I finished my finals, and the biggest surprise came during the social studies test. As I was reading the directions, I stumbled upon something unexpected... The directions said, "If you want to opt out of taking the test and get 100%, all you have to do is put your name and date at the top of the paper, then get out a book and silently read."

I couldn't believe it at first, but it was right there in black and white. I followed the instructions, put my name and date at the top, and grabbed a book. Looking around, I noticed a few others had also caught onto the directions, but there were quite a few who hadn't read them and were taking the 50- question test.

What surprised me even more was that the teacher seemed to be smiling, as if this was part of her plan. It felt like a classic case of trickery but in a fun and unexpected way.

Later in science class, Benji mentioned that his dad signed him up for the swim team, and he's genuinely excited about it! It's awesome to see his enthusiasm about joining.

Overall, what a way to wrap up finals week! Unexpected turns and surprises sure kept things interesting.

Ready to cruise through the last few days!

Jane

-x-X-x-X-x-X-x-X-x-X-x-X-x-X-x-

June 13th

Dear Diary,

Field Day was an absolute blast, the perfect way to wrap up the school year!

At first, I have to admit, the bounce house the school got seemed a tad babyish, but that didn't stop my friends and me from bouncing like there was no tomorrow. Harold what is showing off like crazy! He was effortlessly doing front and back flips. It looks like all the time on his diving board paid off. I'm pretty sure even Janey was impressed.

Then there was the inflatable obstacle course. I might not have been the most graceful competitor, but I was super fast! Racing through that course, stumbling and laughing—that's what made it so fun, despite my lack of skill. I even got to race against my math teacher, who didn't stand a chance.

And let's not forget the face painting! Janey and Alejandra went for a beautiful glitter garden

while I chose a neon pink tiger. Harold cracked us up with a pirate look which included a headband, eye patch, and beard stubble.

And to top it all off, we indulged in some ice cream and pizza. It was the perfect way to end our sixth-grade year in style—with full bellies and huge smiles on our faces.

Field day was a mix of laughter, games, and shared moments with friends. It was a fantastic way to celebrate the end of the school year, creating memories that will last a lifetime.

Wishing I could relive today again, and again, and again...

Jane

-x-X-x-X-x-X-x-X-x-X-x-X-x-X-x-

June 15th

Dear Diary,

The last day of school is always bittersweet, and today was no exception. The school handed out the yearbooks, and flipping through it was a trip down memory lane. As I went through the pages, I couldn't help but reflect on how this year had gone.

In my mind, there were moments where I felt like I was really struggling to find my place, but looking back now, I realize I've grown so much and made some amazing friends along the way. It's funny how my perspective has changed with time.

One photo in particular caught my eye. It was a snapshot of me and Harold laughing at our locker. It might seem small, but it represents a lot. Harold became more than just a locker partner; he became a friend.

A wave of emotions hit me when I stumbled upon a candid photo of Alejandra and me at lunch. Our friendship hasn't always been a smooth ride—there were crushes, drama, and moments that tested our bond. But here we are, at the end of the year, stronger than ever.

There's also a picture of the robotics team. That was an adventure in itself. Robotics turned out to be something I really liked. There was this satisfaction in creating and problem- solving that I hadn't experienced before. Sure, it took some time to get into the swing of things, but once I did, it was an amazing feeling.

The most astonishing realization hit me when I thought about how Janey and I had become friends. From initial feelings of envy to the beautiful friendship we formed, it's been an unexpected journey. The last photo I stumbled upon showcased Alejandra, Janey, Harold, and me dancing on stage during the talent show. It encapsulated the spirit of our friend group perfectly!

As I look back on my sixth-grade year through the pages of the yearbook, it's amazing to see how much I've grown. There were uncertainties, challenges, and totally embarrassing fails but I found my place, forged friendships, and discovered new passions.

The summer ahead feels like a canvas waiting to be painted with new adventures. I can't contain my excitement! In just two weeks, my cousin Dominique will arrive, and we've made plans to dive into our diary entries, reflecting on our first year in middle school. It's going to be so much fun reliving (most of) those moments and seeing how much we've changed and grown.

Seventh grade is just around the corner, and I wonder what it has in store for me. There's this thrilling mix of anticipation and curiosity about what new friendships, challenges, and discoveries await. I'm ready to begin another chapter, armed with the lessons and experiences from this year.

The future feels full of possibilities, and I can't wait to see where the journey takes me.

I made it through sixth grade!

Jane

If you loved Jane's adventure, take a peek at her cousin Dominique's diary:

Unique Dominique

Has To Take a Backseat

September 1st

Hello Journal!

My name is Dominique McKiddy! I'm an eleven-year-old going into middle school this year. Buckle up, because my summer was a whirlwind! It all started when I took my first-ever plane ride to the land of sunsets and surf. My Aunt Erica's place on the West Coast turned out to be a home away from home!

Life was different there but in the best possible way. I shared a room with my cousin Jane and it was like meeting my long-lost twin! My other cousins (Jane's younger brothers) Joey and Carl made it feel like we were part of a circus, but the cool kind with acrobats and magic tricks.

Jane and I joined the swim team (spoiler: I'm not exactly the next Olympic swimmer, but hey, I made waves... literally). Chlorine became our perfume, and the pool became our watery kingdom where we chased dreams of gold medals and synchronized dives.

Then came the epic road trip! We zoomed to the big city in Uncle Drew's car. The skyscrapers towered like giants, and we stayed in a hotel straight out of a fancy magazine. We pretended we were celebrities hiding in the heart of the urban jungle. It was so much fun!

In the city, I stumbled into a shop where I found two beautiful journals. That's when I had an incredible idea: Jane and I should document our first year of middle school! I gave Jane a journal the day before I flew back to the East Coast. And you know what? She loved it! We pinkie-promised to pour our hearts into these journals, and when we reunite next summer, we'll share our epic year of sixth grade.

It's like sending messages in a bottle across the sea of time!

Ready for the good, the bad, and the ugly!

Dominique

~O~O~O~O~O~O~O~O~O~O~O~

September 3rd

Hey Journal,

Today I'm off on another weekend escapade to suburbia. Yep, my Dad is swooping in to whisk me away for some quality father-daughter shenanigans. My parents divorced when I was four years old, so I split my time between my mom and dad. But guess what? My life is pretty awesome.

Most of the time I live with my mom in the city. We live in a super cozy townhome. My room? It's a museum of memories and dreams... a haven where posters tell stories, fairy lights dance like fireflies, and every stuffed animal has its own VIP spot. My mom is the superhero here! She grants me the freedom to paint my world in every shade of "Dominique."

Every other weekend I go to Dad's suburban kingdom. His house is like a sprawling palace straight from a fairy tale! My room there? Picture-perfect, like something out of a film set. It's huge!

It's not just me and Dad in that giant house. Five years ago, Dad married Rayna, and she's become an essential part of my weekend extravaganzas. Now, I'm not just Dominique, daughter of Valerie and Rob. I'm also the step-daughter to Rayna, and step-sister to Hailey, a pint-sized bundle of energy.

Mom's place is at the heart of the city's rhythm, where the streets hum with life and friends are a skip away. Dad's place? It's a serene pause, a place where newness sparkles.

Ready for some suburban serenity.

Dominique

September 4th

Hey Journal,

Today I ended up with a sprinkle of unexpected glitz! It started with Dad, Rayna, Hailey and I going to a local shopping center. Dad ran into a restaurant so he could buy a gift card for a friend's birthday, leaving the ladies to do some exploring.

Now, let me paint the scene: a shopping center buzzing like a beehive. Our wandering led us to this charming little store with an array of shiny accessories. Rows upon rows of jewelry, hairclips, bags, and anything else a girl might need to spruce up her look.

In this glittery paradise, I saw a poster saying they had 25% off ear piercings that day. That's when I knew I had to get my ears pierced! A sprinkle of courage and a dollop of pleading turned into a full-blown campaign to convince Rayna to say "yes."

She agreed, but there was a catch: I needed the green light from Dad! As if on cue, Dad walked into the store. At first, he seemed a bit hesitant when the idea of piercing my ears came up, but Rayna stepped in, assuring him that I was responsible enough to get it done. Eventually, he agreed, but with the condition that Mom was also okay with it.

I pulled out my cell phone and called Mom. The conversation buzzed with talk of needles, earrings, and the importance of keeping the piercings clean. Then, the verdict came through the phone line. A "yes!"

Dad flagged down a staff member who fetched the piercer. They delved into all the necessary paperwork while I perched in that chair, poised for the 'magic' to begin. And there it was—a tiny (but painful) pinch on each earlobe followed by the sweet victory of freshly pierced ears! I felt like a warrior princess, adorned with newfound courage and golden happy-face studs that matched the smile on my face.

Ready to show off my cute earrings in middle school!

Dominique

~O~O~O~O~O~O~O~O~O~O~O~

Labor Day, September 5th

Hey Journal,

This morning I eagerly waited for Mom to come pick me up. When she arrived and caught sight of the glittering studs adorning my ears, she gave me the biggest smile. From what I could tell she loved them. I said bye to Dad, Rayna, and Hailey (I hate saying bye to her) and then Mom and I were off to the city!

On the way home, we got hungry so a fast-food frenzy ensued. In the sacred realm of burgers and fries, we had a conversation about middle school. Mom was a fountain of advice as we navigated the topics of lockers, homework, and teachers. She's my compass in this sea of uncertainties and I'm glad I got to talk with her.

After our meal, we drove home and I dashed four townhouses over to see Sophia! She's my secret weapon for conquering middle school. I went into her too purple room and together, we unleashed our creativity and concocted the most jaw-dropping first-day outfits!

In Sophia's room, amidst the fabrics, colors, and laughter, we schemed and planned. A dash of glitter here, a pop of color there, and voilà! We're going to be the fashion icons of Golden Springs Middle School!

Tomorrow, middle school opens its gates. I'll stride in, brandishing my new piercings, an amazing outfit, and armed with Mom's wisdom.

Till then, soaking up the last rays of the Labor Day sun.

Dominique

~O~O~O~O~O~O~O~O~O~O~O~

September 6th

Hey Journal,

Today my middle school journey officially commenced! I woke up instantly when my alarm went off. I was buzzing with excitement as I put on my blue skirt, flower pattern t-shirt, and denim jacket that screamed 'cool.' A pair of white tennis shoes tied the look together. I also spent extra time styling my red curls to perfection. By the time I walked out the door I looked flawless!

At the bus stop, Sophia was there in the outfit we picked for her. She wore wide-legged jeans and a cute tank top with a heart pattern. Her straight blonde locks had a handful of cute clips that framed her face perfectly. She radiated confidence!

The bus picked us up and I could tell people were checking us out! We walked to the back of the bus like it was our own personal catwalk! Fifteen minutes later we were at the school. We made our entrance with heads held high. All eyes were on us as we made our way to the auditorium.

Once eight o'clock hit, Principal Granger stepped onto the stage and gave his speech. I'm not going to lie, I could barely keep my eyes open as he droned on about school rules. Then came the moment of reckoning—the teachers took the stage. One by one, they read through their homeroom roster. I was heartbroken when Sophia was called into Mr. Peterson's homeroom, and I was left sitting alone.

After what felt like forever, I was finally called by a teacher named, Mrs. Mayo. Even though her name is ridiculous, she is way cool! She led us to her room which was decorated nicely and she even had little gift bags for every student!

The craziness continued as we tumbled into the hallways to find our lockers. My locker? Right next to my homeroom teacher's door in the middle of the hallway. The perfect spot!

I went back to Mrs. Mayo's room and then came the big reveal: my schedule. After my four

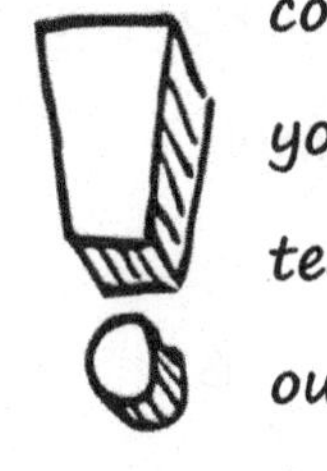

core classes, I have music and PE! Can you believe it? My electives are a dream team of fun. The bell rang and I burst out of homeroom, ready to tackle my first day.

Each class felt like a glimpse into a different universe, but there was this theme, you know? Every teacher went over boring rules like a broken record, and don't even get me started on those cringeworthy icebreakers. I probably told 20 truths and 10 lies, but hey, at least it wasn't tedious schoolwork.

I felt major disappointment when I discovered that Sophia and I only had PE together. Major bummer, right? I mean, we're the ultimate team, so it's going to be hard to get used to classes without her. During PE we began planning for the next term, promising ourselves that we'd synchronize our electives.

Overall, I'd say today has been a major success! Sure, there were some hiccups along the way, but that's what makes middle school exciting!

Let's do this, middle school!

Dominique

About the Author

Allison Felten is a dedicated educator from Portland, Oregon, with over a decade of teaching experience. Outside of the classroom, she finds inspiration in her two canine companions and explores the natural beauty of the Pacific Northwest. Allison explores the power of family, friendship, and self-discovery. This book continues her literary journey centered on delivering high-quality stories for middle-grade readers.

Follow on Facebook

Allison Felten, Author

Check out my author website!

allisonfelten.com

Follow on Instagram

Author_amfelten

Books by this Author

The School Founder's Quest

Book One of the Cursed Corridor Series

After being pulled into a magical vortex, Ralphie find himself solving a paranormal mystery etched in the school's past.

The Timebound Bond

Book Two of the Cursed Corridor Series

Ralphie travels back in time with his new stepsister, Elaura, in order to find a magical artifact that will save their family.

Secrets of the Dream Academy

Book Three of the Cursed Corridor Series

Ralphie and Elaura travel to the 1960s where they team up with twins. Can they discover why students are losing their memories.

Made in the USA
Monee, IL
02 December 2024

71342976R00115